# THE WRECK OF THE TEN SAIL

TIDES OF FORTUNE: BOOK 2

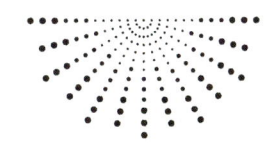

STEVEN BECKER

THE WHITE MARLIN PRESS

Copyright © 2015 by Steven Becker
All rights reserved.
No part of this book may be reproduced in any form or by any electronic or mechanical means, including information storage and retrieval systems, without written permission from the author, except for the use of brief quotations in a book review.

∽

Join my mailing list
and get a free copy of my starter library:
First Bite

Click the image or download here: http://eepurl.com/-obDj

# CHAPTER ONE

STEVEN BECKER

THE WRECK OF THE *Ten Sail*

I stood at the helm watching the crew. At the starboard rail, Lucy and Rory knelt on the deck cleaning the freshly caught dolphin fish. All was quiet now that the thrill of escaping the naval vessel had passed. I watched as the vibrant blue and silver of the dolphin fish faded to a dull green.

Turning to port, I saw Blue staring out to sea, his brow furrowed and jaw clenched. The diminutive African some called a pygmy always sensed things before the rest of us. I called over to him.

"What do you see?" I asked. In truth, I had been watching the same horizon and had seen nothing. Blue shook his head, turned from the rail, and came to stand next to me.

"Mr. Nick," he said, stealing another glance toward the water, "something bad comes."

I followed his gaze, wondering if there was another ship on the horizon. Our lone spyglass was stashed in a small compartment beside the wheel. I reached for it and, with the tube extended, I surveyed the vacant sea and came up empty except for a school of flying fish chased by an unknown predator below.

There was nothing alarming, but I respected Blue's judgment enough to take action.

"Rhames, Mason, to the wheel," I called.

Rhames, the first mate, approached first and silently nodded to me. I eyed his recently shaved beard and shortened hair. It might have concealed his former pirate life to some, but his eyes would always betray his past to me.

Mason approached next. He didn't have a position in the crew, but he had been aboard the ship longer than all of us. We had rescued him from slavers' chains in this very ship's hold when we had been forced to take her in the Shark River. A man of learning, Mason had proven his value many times over since then, and we had become close friends.

"Blue says something bad is out there." I tried to use the same words, hoping that they might pick up a hidden meaning that was lost on me. They both looked past the African and shook their heads.

"Got me what the little bugger sees," Rhames said, "but he's usually right."

Mason and I exchanged glances.

"It's clear for miles," I said.

The whole thing struck me as strange. It was late spring. The weather was alternating between cold fronts with clear skies and a north wind or a southeast breeze bringing warmer, more humid air with thunderheads in the afternoon. But now the weather was indeed unnatural: the wind easterly and the air heavy with humidity.

I was about to voice my observation, when from nowhere, a line of high, thin clouds became visible to the east.

"There. There, Mr. Nick." Blue pointed.

We all knew it then. From our experience, the clearer the sky and higher the clouds, the worse the storm. From what I was looking at, this would be a bad one.

"It's a good month early for a hurricane," Mason said.

Rhames nodded in agreement.

"It might be early, but we can't ignore the signs." We were in a bad spot to be caught in a storm. Halfway between Key West and Cuba in the center of the treacherous Gulf Stream. This was no place to ride out a blow. The prevailing current, moving at six knots to the east, would collide with the storm moving in the opposite direction. We needed to find a protected harbor.

"Havana's not far," Rhames said, reading my mind.

"We're surely dead and certainly broke the minute we sail into that harbor," Mason warned.

He was right. Even though we had renounced our ways, we would certainly be cast as pirates and our ship searched. It wouldn't help that our hold still bore half of Gasparilla's treasure, the better portion stolen from Spanish galleons, enough for ten crews to live a pirate's life. But I was running short on answers. The string of reefs to the east of the harbor would wreck us, and with a storm coming, there would be no way to navigate the western coast.

"I'm thinking we get in close to land to the west of the harbor and get out of the current. Then we can beat around the tip of the island and take shelter in the lee," Mason said.

Rhames and I concurred, and the three of us stood in a trance as the line of clouds approached faster than we thought possible. I called all hands to deck and ordered our sails changed.

Blue's wife, Lucy, had named the ship for the beast that had almost claimed my life deep in the interior of Florida. Despite the coming storm, I couldn't help but smile at the sight of the forty-two-foot, two-masted schooner bearing my totem—the *Panther* —groaning and surging through the waves.

An hour later, land came into view and I turned a few more degrees to the west to give plenty of leeway. We rounded the tip of the island and felt the seas change as the current moved behind us and land blocked the waves. But, despite the calmer water, the line of clouds was closer now and the wind howled at nearly thirty knots. Even in the lee of the island and out of the Gulf Stream, we were in a dangerous position.

"Well?" I asked Mason, who was studying a chart under the cover of the passageway.

"The Gulf of Batabano will give us shelter. I've never been there, but we have little choice now. Clear the land and turn to the east," he said and stashed the chart before a gust could take it from his hands.

We beat into the wind and cleared the western tip of the island before the brunt of the storm hit us. Without the protection of the landmass, we would have certainly been wrecked. Even now, in safer waters, the waves crashed over the gunwales, drenching the decks as we plowed ahead. It was hard going, but we were a seasoned crew. After spending the past few months evading a US Navy frigate, a storm was a simple matter. The sails were reefed, allowing only enough canvas to keep our heading. In this fashion we intended to ride out the blow; there was no outrunning it. We would be wet, but, so long as the bow pointed into the waves, we would survive.

Several hours later, the edge had come off the wind and we were about to turn to port and enter the bay to the north when we saw the sails. This was no weather for a merchant to leave port and by the lines of the ship and cut of the canvas, it wasn't Spanish. That meant only one thing—pirates.

I almost laughed at the irony, but we had to move fast. "Full sail," I yelled to the men still huddled in the companionway. They ran towards their stations, not one hesitating at my command.

"Good catch," Mason said as he joined me at the helm. "Should be enough water between us to outrun 'em."

Rhames yelled to the men to hurry with the rigging, then strode over to join us. "Lot of open water out there," he said as he took the spyglass from me. The pirate ship was under full sail and steadily closing the gap. "Don't know her, but we've not been this far south in years."

Suddenly a loud bang came from the rigging and the ship lurched forward. I turned to starboard, and with full sails, the *Panther* heeled onto her side and picked up speed. For a moment I struggled against the weather helm, the bow pulling towards the wind, but I turned the wheel off a few degrees before either of the men had a chance to correct me.

"Fastest course to nowhere is our best bet," Mason said.

"Aye," Rhames agreed. "Gotta outrun 'em."

As I let the wind fill the sails, I felt the *Panther* rise in the water and pick up speed. With that kind of wind and under full sail, she should have been making another knot or two. Still, we were faster and I could see the pirate sails gradually becoming smaller. We sped on for many miles, but then our ship began to slow as if it were dragging an anchor. The schooner was becoming increasingly difficult to steer, but when I looked back, I saw that our pursuer had already vanished over the horizon.

"What's ahead?" I asked, still gripping the spokes of the wheel. Mason patted me on the shoulder and left the quarterdeck to go for a chart. Rhames moved closer.

"That was nice work, Nick," he said, and although still shaken, I suppressed a grin.

It was Rhames who had initially backed me as captain after our pirate ship, the *Floridablanca*, had been sunk by the Navy in a ruse near Gasparilla Island. I was a young seventeen-year-old cabin boy then, learning everything I could from our captain, the legendary Gasparilla. When he fell, I had led our group out of the wilds of Florida, through the uncharted Everglades and into the Keys. Now a sturdier eighteen, I felt like I had gained a lifetime of experience.

However, I was reminded of my naivety when Mason came back with the chart and called Rhames over to spread it onto a nearby table. I yelled for Swift to take the wheel and joined the two men hovering over the chart.

Mason moved his finger from Cuba towards the open water, showing our course towards a small island a hundred miles away with two smaller landmasses to the east. Beyond them was Jamaica, a place I wanted no part of. Word had come up the Florida coast over the last year or so that the British were clearing out the old pirate haunts of the island. To the west lay Mexico and the Bay of Campeche, another pirate haven.

I was about to ask about the island called Grand Cayman when I heard a scream from the galley and Rory stormed onto deck, "We're taking on water. We're sinking!"

## CHAPTER TWO

### STEVEN BECKER
### THE WRECK OF THE Ten Sail

I ran to the hold, cursing myself for not investigating when I felt the boat slow. Mason left Swift at the helm and followed me down the ladder, almost running into me when I stopped abruptly. It was near night and hard to see into the hold, but I could hear the water sloshing against the bulkhead. When I descended another step, I felt the water.

"Rhames! Get some hands to the pumps," I yelled as I slid the rest of the way down the ladder into the darkness. Waist-deep in water, I waded to the pump and started working furiously.

"Easy, Nick," Rhames said when he joined me and took the handle. "Ain't gonna do no good to work faster than the pump. Just burn yourself out."

I left the pumping to him and the other men and went in search of the source. Carefully I opened the hatch to the bilge.

I wasn't ready for the rush of water that swept me off my feet and pushed me back toward the main hold. Struggling to my feet, I fought my way into the bilge, now accessible, as the water had leveled throughout the entire lower deck. And I found the leak.

Even in the dark of the hold I could see and feel the water

pouring in through the deck boards of the keel. I had no idea how it had happened. Maybe we had struck a log, or the force of slamming into the waves had pried the caulking from the boards. We had been running hard for close to a month now, taking no time for repairs. Whatever the cause, at the moment it didn't matter—all that did was how to fix it.

Careening the vessel was the only proper solution, but with the treasure aboard and no habitable land nearby, I had to find another way. I climbed out of the bilge, passed the men furiously working the pumps, and went up the ladder to the deck.

"She's pulling to the weather. Damn hard to steer," Swift said through gritted teeth, the sinews on his forearms standing proud as he gripped the wheel.

From the set of the sails, I knew he had eased the sheets and turned away from the wind. Clearly, the added weight was causing trouble. We would need the entire crew below decks to solve the problem. I grabbed a section of stout line and brought it to the helm.

"We need to tie off the wheel and fix the leak," I said. "Hold her tight."

I tied a bowline knot to the rail, and into the free end of the line I tied a cinch knot with a loop, quickly feeding the end through the wheel. *This is the tricky part*, I thought, as I brought the bitter end back through the loop. If Swift lost control of the wheel, my arm would be pulled into the spokes. I drew a breath and pulled hard on the end. The mechanical advantage provided by the loop tightened the line and I tied several half-hitches before exhaling.

We stood back and watched the line strain against the load of the ship, but it held. I checked our course, glancing ahead to make sure there were no obstacles, then called everyone down into the hold, carrying a lantern ahead of me.

"Bloody lot of water," someone said as we waded to the bilge.

The pumps had kept us afloat, but from the look of the men

taking turns, the sweat dripping from their bodies, we could not keep up the pace.

I directed the men's attention to the boards. "Something's happened to the keel," I said. "The lot we took her from didn't do much in the way of taking care of her. Should have had a better look before we crossed."

Mason took the light and went down into the bilge, calling back a minute later that I was right. The tropical salt water was hard on even the hardest oak, and boats were routinely careened, cleaned, and recaulked to prevent exactly this. I looked around at the dark hold, lit only by the lantern. It was full night now and the moon would not rise for several hours.

"Bring the light up," I called down to Mason.

He emerged from the bilge and handed me the lantern. I scanned the chests and crates, looking for anything that might serve. We could drape a sail over the keel and let the pressure of the water seal the leak, but the seas were still churned up from the storm, making it impossible to set the sail in place. The repair would have to be made from within.

"Cotton," I called out.

Everyone's eyes shifted to me. They knew instantly what I had in mind, and their first instinct was not to waste valuable cargo.

"Back to the pumps," I yelled, turning their attention to the task at hand. "If we can't hold out the water, there'll be no spending the money anyway." I conjured up my best pirate speak. "Ain't no brothels at the bottom of the sea."

Mason was already one step ahead of me. He had grabbed the closest crate, prying off the top with his huge hands. He pulled out the fluffy rolls of material, grabbed an armful, and headed into the bilge. I grabbed what I could carry and went after him. Rory was down with us now and held the light as we frantically stuffed the material into any crack we could find. When we finally took a break, I noticed my fingers were torn and swollen, but, for the first time, the water had receded from our waists to our knees. It was working. For how long I didn't know.

I left the bilge and called out to Rhames to cut the pump crew and have the other men help stuff cotton into the deck boards. Although the material was porous when spread out, when compressed, it held the shape of the cavity and barely wept water. In a few minutes the hold would be clear.

I was about to applaud our efforts when suddenly, we all lost our footing. The boat took a sudden course change, the result of an accidental jibe. Without the weight of the water, her trim had changed and we were beam to the seas, in danger of capsizing.

I bounded up the ladder with Mason and Rory on my heels. Reaching for my dagger, I ran to the helm, told them to step back, and cut the line holding the wheel. It snapped and released the wheel. I struggled to take control of the ship and finally turned us into the wind. Slowly she came about and the sails filled.

"That's the luck of you," Rory spat. "Escape a pirate ship only to nearly sink us."

My smile of relief faded at the reproach. Dumbstruck, I watched her walk away.

I felt a hand on my back as Mason tried to offer some comfort. "Never mind the girl," he said. "We need to get this rot-infested hull onto a beach, and soon."

I watched Rory return below and wondered why she had such an effect on me. Mason was right, though. I needed to focus on the task at hand.

"We're going to have to stay on this course or the leaks'll just start all over again," I said. "She can't take the pounding of the seas."

I called an order to the men and turned the wheel to starboard, pointing the bow due south. The sails were trimmed to the new course and the deck settled as the bow cut easily through the waves. "For better or worse, our course is set. Where do you reckon it'll lead?"

Mason glanced at the compass and took the chart in his hands. Using dead reckoning, he calculated our position and course. "Expect we'll be eating turtle on Grand Cayman sometime the day after tomorrow."

I glanced over his shoulder at the chart and saw the small island set alone in the sea, flanked by her two smaller sisters, Cayman Brac and Little Cayman to the east. I knew little of the islands other than they were named for the crocodiles, or *caimans*, there in abundance and were under British control. And with no major ports or industry that I was aware of, I assumed they were loosely governed. This could be good or bad, but we needed a beach to repair the ship and would have to suffer whatever consequences our choice brought. At least we were sailing away from the sure danger of Jamaica. I focused on the feel of the boat for a minute and called an order to the men in the rigging to help settle the ship. Once done, I allowed them back on deck, where they collapsed, exhausted.

I stayed on the wheel for several hours watching the storm move away and the seas settle into gentle rollers. Rhames came up from the hold and reported the bilge was dry and the ship returned to its typical night watch schedule. Near the bow, silhouetted by the rising moon, I could see the outline of Blue and Lucy sharing a pipe. I gave Swift instructions for the watch and passed him the wheel.

I went to go below when I saw Rory coming onto the deck. Her words still stung and I turned towards the hold to hide. Too late. She called to me.

"A word, Nick?" Her voice rang sweeter than before.

I looked in her direction, and when I saw the moonlight on her face and her freshly brushed hair, I forgot her earlier words. I went towards her and she guided me to an empty spot near the stern.

"I'll apologize for what I said earlier," she said in the way that a woman says something to make peace, but doesn't really mean it.

I was helpless around her. I nodded.

"I saw you with the chart. Where're we headed?"

"South," I said coyly.

She smacked my arm and waited.

"Cayman Islands. We need a beach to careen the boat and make some repairs."

Rory turned to me. The look on her face was one I'd seen once before, but now I wondered what it meant.

## CHAPTER THREE

STEVEN BECKER

THE WRECK OF THE
*Ten Sail*

We were into the afternoon of the next day when one of the men in the rigging spotted land. The island was just a faint line on the horizon, but the clouds holding above indicated it was indeed our destination. The problem now was time. Mason knew of the island, but had never been there himself, and the chart showed little detail save for a deadly ring of reefs surrounding the landmass. Approaching after dark would be too risky.

The men wouldn't be happy about having to man the pumps overnight, but there was little else to do. I ordered the topsails furled and the mains reefed to slow our progress. I scrapped the night watch and called everyone on deck. Mason and I split the night and I added a rotation of men on the pumps.

This close to an unknown shore, extra precautions would be needed. I sent two men to the bow to work in shifts, one watching the other on the lead. Now at our posts, the silence was unnatural. Everyone was quiet, listening for the sound of surf breaking on the shoreline or a shoal. A sound any man on a ship dreaded, especially at night.

At dawn we heard the unmistakable sound of water hitting land and all hands came on deck to watch. The lead had still not struck bottom, but there, not a quarter mile away, was land. I left the wheel to Mason and climbed the rigging for a better vantage point from which to watch our approach. From near the top of the main mast, the water was the deepest blue I had ever seen, but the land was hellish. Jagged grey rocks extended into the water, offering no approach to the island. I yelled down to Mason to turn to starboard, hoping the western shore would be better protected from the trade winds and perhaps host a beach to careen the ship.

We crossed the entrance to a bay and I thought about seeking refuge there, but the clear water guarding its entrance told me it was shallow. Smoke rose in a column, suggesting there was a settlement there. Maybe we could go undetected, but the risk was not worth it. Past the bay I could see the land curl to the south and I relayed the information to Mason. The sails swung from a dead run to a beam reach as he changed course to follow the shoreline. I soon forgot the smoke, when, around the point, I saw the brilliant white sand stretching for miles.

As we approached the crescent-shaped beach, I climbed down and went to the bow. "Anything on the lead yet?" I asked Red.

"Not a thing," he answered, and tossed the weight again.

We were close to shore now, closer than I would have liked without knowing the area. I scanned the deck for Blue. The pygmy had a sixth sense about these things. I found him in the rigging on the foremast.

"What do you think?" I called up to him.

"Is good," he yelled back.

That was enough for me. Provided the bottom eventually showed itself, the spot was perfect. From the rigging, one could see the bay over the thin landmass. An attack would be easy to spot. Fresh water might be a problem, but we had several casks in the hold that would last several days, long enough to make the repairs we needed.

I heard the man on the line call out twenty fathoms and looked over the rail. The bottom was still invisible and we were within spitting distance of the beach. He called ten fathoms and the color changed drastically to a clear green. Rocks and coral became visible.

"Drop anchor," I yelled.

The men in the rigging dropped sail, the chain slid through the cleats, and I waited for it to grab. Not ten feet from shore, the hook caught and swung us stern to the beach, the waves crashing right behind us. I lined up two palm trees in the distance and waited several minutes to see if we drifted. The ship held. I let out a sigh of relief.

Careening a boat in the best of circumstances was hard work. In northern latitudes one only had to beach the boat at high tide and wait for the water to recede, but this close to the equator the tides were only about a foot in difference. Everything would have to come off the ship and then we would undergo the strenuous process of hauling her masts. We could only hope they could take the stress and not break when we pulled them to the ground and rolled the hull onto its side. Fortunately there were some large palm trees within fifty feet of the shoreline we could use to anchor the ground tackle.

I posted a watch while Rhames quickly organized the men into groups and started the tedious process of unloading.

"Cannon first," I called to him. She was a light ship with only four carronades—two on each rail. I marked the sand where I wanted them: one facing in each direction at forty-five-degree angles to the water so any approach by land would be covered. The other two were to be faced towards the sea at an angle that would have them hit any ship attempting to board us. Lucy and Blue came towards me, both carrying blowguns, and I nodded without a word. They would find food and water.

The cannon were unloaded and set in place with a keg of powder and shot beside them. The next chore was to offload the cargo. Using the boom, we rigged a block and pulley to ease the work of lifting the crates and chests from the hold. Everything was then set on the beach and inspected for water damage. The storm had ruined at least a third of the trade goods: cotton, fabric, and foodstuffs. Last to come off were the chests holding what remained of Gasparilla's treasure. We had only half of what we had originally departed with, but even that filled two large chests and would ensure us all a life of leisure if we could ever get anywhere safe enough to spend it.

We had lost a good part of it in the mouth of the Charlotte River when one of the boats had gone down, and another two chests were buried on a small island in the Florida Keys, but the US Navy patrolled those waters and, to their eyes, we were pirates. So there it would remain, at least until we could clear our names and were welcome in American waters.

Rory came towards me as I directed the last crate to its resting place. "You've been ignoring me."

I had been. It was her questions I was avoiding, her persistent prodding about the future.

"I don't have the answers you're looking for," I said. When she moved to interrupt, I raised my hand. "First we fix the ship. Then we figure out our next step." I was in no mood for another argument.

She sensed my fatigue and backed down. "Just tell me how to help," she said.

"We need firewood."

Without a word she walked toward the tree line. I heard footsteps approaching as I watched her go, and my gaze lingered on the jungle long after she disappeared. Why was everything with her so hard? Several seconds passed before I realized Rhames was standing next to me waiting for orders.

"Can I suggest we send a scout in both directions?" he asked. "Have 'em walk the beach until dark and then come back. That'll give them about an hour, enough to cover a few miles before they turn around. Get a sense of what's out there."

"Right, then," I said, glad for the interruption. "From the rigging I could see the bay is not a hundred yards through the trees. Maybe we ought to set a watch there to make sure no one comes at us from that direction."

"Aye. I'll handle it, then. I see you got your hands full with the girl." He grinned and walked away.

There were only three of us left on the beach now, and with darkness coming, I went after Rory to help with the firewood. As I approached the tree line, she came out with an armful and we walked in silence back to the beach. We made several trips between the jungle and the pile before she spoke.

"You know I'm not looking to fight all the time. I can help you if you just let me," she said.

"I can't get past tomorrow, never mind cast our future for you," I said.

"I have some ideas," she said. "Maybe we can talk later." Then she turned and walked back towards the brush.

I moved to follow her when the sound of an animal slithering through the brush caught my attention, and I realized why we had seen no sign of man.

The caiman's eyes glowed in the twilight as it stalked her. I took a few steps backward to look for a weapon and it turned its beady eyes on me. For every wary step backwards I took toward the safety of the beach, the caiman shuffled its four small legs and, with blinding speed, ate up the distance. We were only feet apart when it snapped its jaws and allowed me a glimpse of the rows of razor-sharp teeth. I stood silently gaping at it. For now it seemed content to hold the ground, but I doubted that would last. With only the dagger in my belt, I sought a diversion.

"Nick," I heard Rory call. I had to keep her away.

The croc's head turned toward her.

"Nick," she called again.

It was confused now, the spell broken, and I did the only thing I could. I threw the firewood towards it, turned, and ran. I had to keep it from her. It came after me faster than I thought possible. I was in the clear of the beach and still it came, its jaws inches from my pumping legs. Just as I dove into the breakers, I heard the gunshot. When I glanced back, Swift was standing over the carcass, musket in hand and a grin on his face.

## CHAPTER FOUR

STEVEN BECKER

# THE WRECK OF THE Ten Sail

After feasting on the caiman, we sat around the fire, watching it slowly burn down to embers. It was warm enough and we didn't want our night vision ruined by flames. The scouts had walked the beach and found settlements in both directions. With men near and the caimans grunting at our backs, we would have to remain cautious. Lucy and Blue had gone farther than the scouts and reported that the thin landmass extended as it turned east. Tomorrow they would take the canoe and explore the bay.

I had just dozed off when I felt Rory next to me.

"Can we talk?"

The dreaded words shook me awake. "Sure," I muttered, and sat up.

"Don't take this too hard. I'm a woman and we think differently. You lot could sleep in the sand and drink rum every night, but I want more from this life."

She had my attention now. I too had been brought up in better circumstances than I found myself in now. I had enjoyed the company of Gasparilla, who was also educated, but I was not a pirate at heart. Besides Mason, the present crew left me wanting. "I have to admit the same," I said.

"You know the problem, then."

I did. "Pirate stench is hard to wash off," I said.

I could see her almost smile in the soft light of the fire. "So we agree."

"Knowing it and knowing what to do about it are two different things. I was brought up with books and numbers, not cutlasses and muskets."

"Then walk away," she urged. "I know the governor here. If it's the same man, maybe he can help."

That was it, then. I remembered the strange look on her face when I'd told her our destination a few days before. Now I sat in silence next to her, wondering what she was after.

~

With the task before us and the lack of rum the night before, we were up at dawn. While the men restarted the fire and ate, Blue and I scouted the brush, collecting branches from the trees. We brought these to a pit that Lucy had dug and lined with dried palm fronds. Inside the pit was a large vessel jammed with sticks and covered with sand. Once the fire started we piled wood on top and left the oven to burn.

The sails were hauled down and laid out on the beach, where Lucy and Rory inspected them for damage, repairing anything that looked suspect. Next the yards were removed and the masts stripped of their rigging. Mason and I hauled the blocks and tackle out to the trees and started rigging them there. A double loop around the base of the stoutest palm provided the support we would need to roll the hull. The rope was run through the tackle, and the men gathered around, ready to pull.

Together we pulled the mast down close to the sand, rolling the ship and exposing the seaward side of the hull. The lines were tied off and we got to work. We were already exhausted from the effort, but we were anxious to get the ship righted as soon as possible. Swift, Red, and Mason rigged scaffolding on the seaward side, allowing us to work out of the water. First, any broken planks were removed and replaced. When this was finished we split into pairs and tended to every board. One man would pry the planks apart while the other stuffed the gap with cotton. When the boards were released, they compressed the cotton, sealing the gap. It took the better part of the morning to seal one side of the hull. We paid special attention to the keel, which had taken the brunt of the damage.

After a break for lunch, we uncovered the pit, cool since the fire had burned out, and took the container it held, now full of pitch, to the ship. There was not enough to coat the entire hull, so we carefully applied the tar to each crack and joint to seal them. By midafternoon the work was done and we relaxed. Tomorrow we would repeat the process on the other side.

I tried to rest, but anxiety ate at me. In another day the *Panther* would again be seaworthy and her crew in need of purpose. In the old days we would just sail off in search of another victim, but I had driven home to the men that their days of plunder and debauchery were over. There were few ports that accepted our kind now, with Port Royal and some other famous haunts being closed by the Crown. The last places still open to pirates were no place we wanted to be. With a crew of eight men and two women, we would be easy prey for the larger bands.

My thoughts were interrupted by a call from the watch, and I saw Red pointing at two ships anchoring just off shore. With men at the seaward cannons, we armed and gathered in a semicircle ready to face the threat.

One of the ships dropped a small dory into the water. Four men climbed in the boat and started rowing for the beach, but they were not my concern. I was studying the schooners holding offshore. They flew the Union Jack, and I wasn't sure if I should be comforted or alarmed. Whatever their intentions, we had no escape. With the careened hull of our ship, four cannon and only a handful of men, we would need to play this very carefully.

"Ahoy," I called towards the men in the dory. One man jumped from the bow and, with the aid of a small wave, pulled the boat onto the beach. The other men jumped out. Although they had cutlasses at their sides, they were not drawn. A well-dressed, older man was last to reach the beach.

"Who's in charge of this lot?" he asked as he came forward.

I stepped forward. "I am." I extended my hand.

He looked at me suspiciously. "This your boat?"

"Aye. We got caught in a storm and she started taking on water," I explained.

"Governor will be wanting to see you." He pointed to the south. "There's a small settlement called Georgetown at the end of the beach. Follow that round and you'll come to Bodden Town. It'd be a bit easier across the bay, though."

Mason and Rhames were by my side now.

"What's to stop us from making repairs and leaving?" I asked.

He set a hand on his cutlass, causing us to do the same, then released it. "Seems you have a bit of work to do there," he said, nodding at our ship.

I acknowledged the threat. We were indeed sitting ducks until the boat was repaired—easy cannon fodder for the two schooners offshore. With only four cannon and a skeleton crew, we could not compete with their guns. Time was our enemy, but if I could stall him until Blue was able to scout out this Bodden Town, we would know what we faced.

"Very well, tell your governor that I'll be seeing him in a day or so."

"Now was what he was thinking," he replied. "We'd be happy to escort you—and the girl, too." He cast a look at Rory.

This was no invitation. The two men in the boat pushed past Rhames and went for Rory. Swift and Mason closed ranks to protect her and I saw Rhames reach behind his back and pull a flintlock pistol. The old pirate was never far from weapons. He leveled the gun in their direction and they backed away.

"We'll be needing no escort. If your governor wants to talk, have him come to us," I said and signaled Swift to grab the man. In one move he had his dagger at the man's throat. "You men," I called to the others. "Go back to your ships and tell your governor that if he wants to talk to me, he can find me here."

They looked at each other and then at their leader. Swift edged the knife closer.

"Go, you fools. Tell him there's pirates on this beach," he gasped.

Two men jumped in the boat and manned the oars while the other pushed off the beach. I watched until they were clear of the surf and pulling hard for the closest schooner.

"Take his weapons and tie him up."

One of the schooners made a move towards the dory and I thought about our next step. I met eyes with Rory, regretting that once again we were on the wrong side of the law. With the prisoner still standing, Rhames tied his hands.

"Make him comfortable," I said. I didn't want any more ill will than I had already created. I walked over to Blue, and together we walked inland, past the tree line to the sparkling bay. After I called to them, Red and Swift followed with the canoe.

Blue was as the stealthiest of any man, but I was not sure if he could evaluate armaments and threats. I needed to go with him to better understand our circumstances. The canoe was ready to launch and Mason joined us at the water, awaiting orders. I told them my plan and assigned cannon placements and watches. We would direct all cannon at the water. If a threat came from the bay, Blue and I would be in a position to see it and alert the camp.

I turned to Mason. "Get the other side repaired quickly. By night if you have to. I have a feeling we may need to make a quick getaway."

"We can turn her before nightfall and work by torchlight on the other side. The tar should be cured by then." He paused.

"What is it?"

"There's a wreck off these waters I've heard of," he said. "Called the Wreck of the Ten Sail. If you can garner any information, I'd appreciate it."

I nodded and jumped in the bow of the canoe and waited for the men to push us into the clear water.

## CHAPTER FIVE

### STEVEN BECKER
### THE WRECK OF THE *Ten Sail*

We sat in a clump of mangroves near the entrance to the bay, I remained low in the bow of the canoe. Blue and I had pulled into the mosquito-infested trees when we saw the first schooner round the point. Surprisingly, she turned into the clear water. I studied her course. Knowing how to navigate the bay could prove important. We stayed under cover until the ship moved past. Land was visible on all three sides of the estuary, so there was no chance of losing sight of her.

We paddled around a small island and turned again to the south. The bay was several miles wide. To my right was the backside of the beach the *Panther* was careened on. To the left I saw only mangroves. Directly ahead was a small town with several ships at anchor. *This must be Bodden Town*, I thought. We moved closer to shore and could soon see the schooner had dropped anchor and the dory was being rowed to a pier. Staying with the shoreline, we cautiously approached the anchorage and I evaluated the settlement that lay ahead.

I could see no fortifications, only several clusters of buildings. Cotton grew in a large farm to the right and cattle grazed to the left. The tips of several larger masts became visible over the landmass as we approached. I guessed that the land was narrow, similar to the beach we had landed on but with a better anchorage on the ocean side. We were clearly looking at the backside of the settlement.

"Stop paddling, Mr. Nick. You make too much noise," Blue whispered as we slid in and out of the protection of the mangroves.

I laid the paddle on the gunwale and continued my observation of the town. The houses were mainly wattle and daub, small rectangular buildings crafted from a sand-and-lime mixture. Their roofs were covered with palm fronds and looked in good repair. Toward the center of the town were several wooden buildings with shake roofs. All the buildings were elevated off the ground as a safeguard against the tidal surge that accompanied the frequent storms.

We continued towards the village where several small boats were anchored. Shirtless men waded in the shallows, bending over, removing something from the bottom and bringing it to the boats. Our boat was a different construction, but it was the same size and I expected it would blend in. Information could only be gained by watching, so I motioned Blue towards a clear area and jumped into the water. I immediately regretted my bare feet. The bottom was covered with jagged rock that cut even my calloused skin. I looked at the other men, who were piling these rocks into their boats, and I bent over to mimic their movements, slowly pulling rocks from the bottom and placing them in the canoe. My hands and feet were cut, but I continued the work, wondering how these men could tolerate it.

"We should move, Mr. Nick," Blue said. "Nothing more to be seen."

I wasn't satisfied. I pointed to a small beach that would be concealed by the mangroves. "Pull the canoe to shore over there. I'll go scout out the town."

"That's a bad idea. I can go," Blue said.

"They might take you for a runaway slave. We can't take that chance. The merchant ships anchored on the ocean side will provide me an excuse if anyone asks. I just hope the men that saw me on the beach remain on their ship."

Blue paddled to a small section of beach and I jumped out. "If I'm not back by moonrise, go back to the ship."

Without looking back, I walked inland, careful to avoid the sharp rocks buried in the sand and regretting that I'd left my boots at camp. Within a few minutes I found myself on a clear and widening path. I stayed to the side to avoid being seen by the handful of small houses lining the road, their large windows wide open to catch the breeze. The road led to the main pier, where there was enough activity that I felt confident walking freely.

To my left I passed a small rock building flanked by several large cannons aimed at the anchorage, the first sign of armaments I had seen. I guessed the residents felt safe from an attack from the bay.

Because of her reefs and fortifications, wise captains gave this small island a wide berth and remained well to sea, only using the island as a landmark on their way around Cuba, where the Gulf Stream would pull them north. There was no fresh water or riches to be gained here anyway. The only mention I had heard of the island was of the turtle trade.

Several men were gathered on the porch of a larger building I took to be a pub. If there was information to be had, this was the place to gather it. I fingered the small silver coins in my pocket, ready to buy a few glasses of rum. Alcohol didn't suit me, but no man had ever turned down a free drink, and after a few they were often very receptive to questions.

I entered and waited for my eyes to adjust to the dimness. Even with the breeze coming through the open windows, it was still sweltering inside. Men were gathered in small groups, some around tables and others leaning on the bar. Another group huddled in a corner on their knees playing dice. I moved in the direction of a single man standing at the end of the bar. He had the look of a local; his sunburnt face and greying beard were shadowed by the wide brim of a hat fashioned from palm fronds. We exchanged nods as I settled a few feet from him and waited for the woman working the crowd to reach me.

"I'll have a glass and another for my friend here," I called to her. She looked up, and my jaw dropped. She was stunningly beautiful, an exotic blend of every culture that had passed these shores. Her pale grey eyes surveyed me, and I couldn't help but want to touch her ivory skin.

"That'll be two shillings," she said with an English accent. I finally blinked, reached into my pocket, and handed her one of the silver coins.

She fingered the coin and passed it to the man next to me for his opinion.

He rubbed the coin between his fingers and then balanced it on one to guess its weight. "I'm guessing that's about right for the drinks," he said and handed it back to her.

I knew differently. The coin was worth a keg, at least, but it was the smallest change our treasure contained, and with a fortune on the beach, I let it pass. She set the beers down in front of us and walked towards the group playing dice at the far end of the room.

The old man nodded. "Where'd you come by that?" he asked.

"Trading, mostly. Did a little wrecking up in the Keys," I said.

He eyed me suspiciously. "Spanish from the look of it. And old. I'd not be far off guessing that came from the Plate Fleet, gone down off the Florida coast in 1715."

I was impressed with his knowledge. "You know your wrecks."

He sipped his beer again. "Done a little salvage to get by when the turtles are thin."

The talk of wrecks made me forget my reason for coming. I thought of Mason's request back at camp.

"Then you know the Wreck of the Ten Sail?" I probed.

A half-cocked gaze answered my question. "Aye. I was on one of those ships that followed the *Convert* onto the reef. 'Twas about thirty years ago. One of King George's sons was aboard, you know."

"Any salvage to be had from it?"

"A bit floated onto the beach. We tried to drag the bottom, but it's the middle of the reef there. The rest is too deep to get at," he said and finished his beer.

"Any rumor of treasure?" I asked.

"Ah, so there you are, young man. Lookin' for treasure, are you? Rumor has it you was pirates."

I swallowed, and the beer stung in my nostril. If he knew who I was, I had to wonder who else did. I glanced around the room, expecting to be in chains at any second, but the other men were talking amongst themselves or engrossed in their dice game.

The old man must have sensed my panic. "Your secret's safe here…if you buy another." He set his glass on the counter.

The girl came over and refilled his mug, looking to me for more silver. I took the last coin from my pocket and held it out to her.

"You could be here a while," she said, taking the coin before turning to her father. "I've seen that look on your face when you starts talking about treasure."

"Go away now, girl," he said to her before he took a sip and turned back to me. "Now where was I?"

I knew he was toying with me, extending the conversation to get another beer, but I was drawn in now. "You were saying about the wreck."

"Aye. There's ten of 'em laying on the reef. The *Ludlow*, which I was on, and eight other merchants led to their death by the *Convert*. We were fifty-eight ships in a convoy from Jamaica, led by that fool of a captain. Wouldn't expect much to be left of the merchants, but the boy, the one that claimed he was Georgie's son, was on the *Ludlow* with me. He couldn't shut up about the silver in her hold. But like I said, she's too deep to get at."

Before he could continue, a shadow moved across the wall and I turned to see two men in the doorway. One looked directly at me and whispered something to the other. I didn't recognize them from the beach, but word must have spread.

The second man left and the first remained by the door, his hand on a pistol stuck in his belt. There were windows on each side of the building and I was about to make a move toward one of them when I felt a tug on my hand. I turned and looked into the eyes of the girl.

"Hurry." She pulled me around the bar and into the back room, saying something about the outhouse loud enough for the man at the door to hear.

She led me out the back door, and before I could ask her anything, she pointed to the brush behind the building. "Best run. They'll have a force out looking for you."

## CHAPTER SIX

### STEVEN BECKER

# THE WRECK OF THE Ten Sail

*I* followed the same path I had taken into the village, running as hard as my injured feet could carry me. Fine crystals of sand ground into my cuts as the small chunks of coral hidden below the surface of the path cut me further. When I heard men behind me, I ran faster. Somewhere between the flashes of pain I realized the futility of my escape. My pursuers had boots and were able to move quickly over the ground, but I was slowing. Even if I could reach Blue and the canoe, we would be easily sighted on the bay and limited to the speed of our two paddles.

It was better to let Blue remain concealed and retreat alone in the dark. I could hide out and make my way overland on the morrow. In the likely event I was captured, we still had the hostage at camp for a bargaining chip.

A shot fired and I felt the bullet zip past me. So much for the hostage, I thought. A flintlock pistol or musket wielded by a running man was far from accurate, so I discounted the threat and ran on. The path ended and I found myself staring at a tangle of mangroves. The ground beneath them looked firm, and with no other option, I ran into the overgrowth.

My foot must have caught on a branch, because the next thing I knew I was face down in the muck. I rolled to the side, hoping to use the cover of the dense growth to conceal myself, when I heard the grunt of the beast. I didn't need to waste any time getting a better look. I knew that sound. I hauled myself to my feet and took off back the way I had come. It would be safer to run into the men than become dinner for the caiman. I heard it shuffle toward me, but three men appeared in front of me and it took off into the brush.

"Well, look what we've got here," one of the men said.

"For a pirate, he doesn't look much," the other added, moving closer.

As they surrounded me and bound my hands, I wondered, was this pirate label never going to wash off of me? Flanked by two men and led by a third, we walked back towards the settlement. I could only hope my men on the beach still held the hostage. Without his life to trade for mine, I could be hanging from a rope by dark.

"Your governor wants to talk to me," I said.

The lead man spat and turned back to me. "That he will, boy. That he will."

My feet were badly hurt and I looked back at the bloody trail I was leaving. Surely Blue would pick up the scent and find me. We reached the settlement and the men took me to the small stone building flanked by the cannon I had seen earlier. The heavy door creaked on its hinges as the lead man pulled it open. I was unceremoniously shoved in and the door closed behind me. I went to the single window, open to the elements but covered with iron bars, and stared out as the men locked the door and walked down the path.

The building was dark, but cool, and it had a bunk built into the back wall. I sat down on the cold stone, knowing my destiny would reveal itself soon enough. I suspected the capture of a pirate would be big news in this sleepy town.

I reviewed my options. My crew was too small to take the village. They might try to break me out, but they would be badly outnumbered and I had no way of knowing if the ship had been made seaworthy. I was limited to trading myself for the hostage or bartering for my freedom.

I crossed one leg over my knee to examine my foot. Several jagged cuts stared back at me. I could have used Lucy's medicine to stave off the infection, but, for the time being, I tore strips from my shirt and fashioned slippers that would at least protect me from further damage. Just as I tied the last strip, I heard men outside the door.

***

"Don't look like no pirate," the governor said.

I stood in front of the governor, less nervous than I expected I would be. I didn't think my looks were going to save me, but one could always hope. My father had been a merchant before our capture by Gasparilla and I had attended many of his meetings. He had taught me to read and write as well as basic mathematics. If I was a pirate, I was an educated one. The more humble I could appear and sound, the less threatening and pirate-like I would be.

William Bodden (I had been informed of his name on the walk over), on the other hand, looked more like a pirate than I did. He was middle-aged, with a muscular build. A beard hid his face and a large pipe extended from his mouth. It was his hair that gave him the look of an outlaw, black with streaks of grey through it, let loose and hanging to his shoulders.

"Let's have it, then, boy. Who are you? Who's your captain and where have you come from? I heard your lot has taken my man hostage. That's not going to go well for ya." He spat out the questions.

I debated whether or not to tell him I was the captain. It could save me or kill me. So I was careful not to overplay my hand. "My name is Nick, sir," I said, knowing a surplus of sirs never hurt anyone. "I am the captain of the vessel careened on the beach. We are merchants making emergency repairs, sir. Hardly pirates."

"Hmm, merchants, you say. Why take the hostage, then? I don't know any merchants to behave like that."

"We've had a hard go of it, sir."

"Or maybe you've something to hide," he said and turned to the sideboard, where he poured two fingers of an amber liquid into a tumbler, then glanced at me, asking without a word if I would join him.

I nodded back. Not because I wanted the drink, but I knew better than to rebuff his courtesy. Gasparilla had taught me as much. Never turn down an offer of hospitality if it's going to prevent a sword through your heart or a bullet in your head. I took the offered glass and waited for the governor to sit. He extended his glass and I copied his gesture. We both drank, him deeply, me just a sip. The fiery liquid was actually quite good; a tinge of honey took the bite out of the rum.

"It seems to me you'd been questioning my authority." He got up and walked to a window. "The king don't take kind to pirates. I could have you in the hold of that ship out there and on your way across the pond. The executioner in the Tower of London would be more than happy to meet you."

There was something about the way he said it that was not sincere. I took another sip of rum and called his bluff. "But you're not going to do that, are you?"

He turned and looked at me. "No, I'm not. At least not on that ship." He pointed out the window to a frigate anchored just offshore. "There's one that passes by here every week or so, though, so you ought to mind your manners. I'd be the judge and jury here. A bit of a forsaken outpost, this rock is, but I make the best of things."

His last sentence aroused both curiosity and fear. It seemed he was going to offer some kind of deal. I sipped again, forgetting myself for a moment and enjoying the spirit.

He stared at me and finished his drink. "Maybe you're a pirate, maybe you ain't. In these waters, you can be a pirate one day and the next you're a privateer."

So that's where he was going. A letter of marque would give us legitimacy. We could sail out of here, wander around the Caribbean for a month or so, and return with the treasure. The governor must have thought of this. It would have to be split with him, surely. But our share would be legal.

"Go on," I said.

"For me to offer you something so valuable, I would need an act of good faith."

"And what would that be?" I asked.

"The release of my man, of course. Then bring your ship here into the harbor and be my guest. Show a bit of trust for your new benefactor."

I didn't have much trust for him, but we were in a bit of a spot. With a letter of marque, the entire British Caribbean would be open to us. I'd grown up Dutch, with no love for the British, but the last I had heard, England controlled most of the islands from the Bahamas to South America. The territory we would be welcome in was vast.

The governor interrupted my thoughts. "This offer ain't open-ended. Repair your ship and be anchored in the harbor by noon the day after tomorrow. If you don't, I'll arrest you as pirates. Escape and I'll spread word of your treachery to every governor in the Caribbean."

# CHAPTER SEVEN

STEVEN BECKER

# THE WRECK OF THE Ten Sail

Heading on a northern course through the bay, I was spellbound. Although the water was several fathoms deep, the bottom appeared only inches away. Stingrays patrolled the sandy floor, and coral heads reached for the surface, breaking the smooth, desert-like bottom.

The governor had offered me dinner and a better bed than the stone bunk in the guardhouse, and in the morning had put me aboard his schooner to take me back to the *Panther*. I hoped the men had worked through the night to complete the work necessary to get her underway. We would need every option at our disposal.

I had already decided to send the hostage back. His usefulness was at an end and the last thing we needed was bad blood with the British. I studied their ship, evaluating how battle-ready it was should we have to face it. Twelve carronades lined the rails, with two smaller guns fore and aft. But, aside from a well-armed ship, I suspected the governor had little power here and no naval presence—just the handful of cannon I had seen by the guardhouse. Still, even though he had little in the way of force, his signature carried the backing of the British Empire. A letter of marque signed by William Bodden would hold the same authority as if signed by the king himself. Conversely, a condemnation from him would end badly for us.

The arguments battled in my mind, but legitimacy won every time. I was a pirate by circumstance alone, having been taken prisoner by Gasparilla's band five years before. It was purely by chance that I was now leading this company. The one act of piracy we had committed was taking a ship from a band of slavers in the Snake River. The attack was brutal, but after freeing Mason and several of his men from the hold, I was able to justify even that. Now I had to convince the crew to give up half our treasure for our own freedom.

The schooner rounded the point and turned to port. We cleared the headland and changed course to the west. I could see our ship in the distance, but we were too far away to tell if she was upright or still careened. While I waited for the ship to close the gap I thought about Blue and hoped he had made it back all right. I had little doubt he had— there were few men capable of tracking him.

The captain gave the order to change our tack and, before I knew it, the anchor was dropped and a crewman pulled the painter attached to the dory towards the stern ladder. I could see the *Panther* clearly now. She was righted and partially rigged. They had indeed been busy while I was gone. A crewman shoved me toward the opening in the rail and I descended the ladder to the awaiting dory. Three well-armed men climbed down behind me. We tossed off the painter and rowed to the beach.

I felt a rush as the small boat surfed the last wave and burrowed its bow in the sand, and I learned something about their seamanship when the next wave took us from behind, pouring water into the boat. I was wet from the waist down when my feet, now clad in borrowed boots, hit the sand.

The cannons were manned and pointed towards us. The

tension was clear, but the crew relaxed when they saw me. I climbed the beach and walked towards Rhames. I would have preferred to talk to Mason first, but Rhames had the backing of the crew as second in command, and I needed to show him the proper respect.

"Nice boots," Rhames said as I drew near. "A bit fancy for my taste."

"All is well," I said. "I had a fine meeting with the governor last night. Release the prisoner and we'll talk about our options."

The crew relaxed visibly when they heard that. Swift brought the man forward, drew his knife, and pulled it in a large arc past the man's throat before cutting the cord that bound his hands.

He gave a push and the man stumbled towards the dory, where the crew helped him aboard. No words were spoken as they waited for a lull in the surf before turning the small boat and rowing hard for deep water before the next wave swamped them. We stood in a cluster on the beach, watching until the dory was past the breakers.

I turned to the group and searched their faces. "Where's Blue?"

Lucy stepped forward, a worried look on her face. "We've not seen him since you left," she said.

If it were any other man, I would have been worried, but Blue's stealth and survival skills were unrivaled. "I'm in need of some of your medicine. We can talk while you have a look at my feet."

We walked as a group to the campfire in the shade of the palm trees. I sat on a log and gingerly pulled the boots from my feet. The bloody pieces of linen fell onto the sand in bits.

Lucy came over and took one foot in her lap. "That's a nasty bit of work you've got there," she said in her unique English accent, part pygmy and part British. "Stay here and I'll fetch my medicine."

Rory came and sat beside me. "Nice work, Captain. You'll be laid up for days. Might we ask how it happened?" Of course she would choose now to scold me.

"What's the report on the ship?" I asked, ignoring her and reasserting my authority.

Mason spoke. "Rigging needs a few more hours, then we'll stow the cargo. She should be ready in the morning."

I knew they had their questions. So, while Lucy tended to my feet, I told the tale of how Blue and I had crossed the bay. I left nothing out, knowing their shrewd minds might pick up something from a detail that I had perhaps missed.

"I think you should trust this man," Rory said when I got to the governor's proposal.

Her comment surprised me. Even though it was one vote in my favor, I didn't like that it had come from her. Still, I laid out my rehearsed argument but saw the doubt on the crew's faces when I finished.

"That's all, then," I said. "My plan would be to do what he asks and get the letter of marque."

A pirate society is democratic, and although I fought the notion that we were pirates, we still held to their rules of government. Rhames was first to disagree, with Swift and Red nodding as he spoke. I fought hard for my point of view—that the value of the letter of marque was worth more than the treasure. After all, I reminded them, we still had the chests buried in the Keys.

"I see your point." Mason said, speaking up for the first time. "We could take up any trade we wanted: wrecking, salvaging, or trade."

The pirates grumbled and I counted their votes. We were nine with Blue missing, but he and Lucy tended to abstain. So with eight votes remaining, I was outnumbered, only being able to count on Rory and Mason. The five remaining pirates would have a quorum.

"Rhames, you've got no loyalties to the Americans, or the British, or the Spaniards. Am I right?" I waited for him to nod. "Pirating is at an end in these waters. Even if you can find a refuge for you and your ill-gotten gains, there'll always be some pauper, jealous of your wealth, who'll turn you in for a small bounty." I paused for effect.

"Adventure is what we are after," I added, now dangling the carrot. "We could take this treasure and split it up. It'll be a fair share for all and enough to live a splendid life, but we'd all die sitting on our arses in some fine house on a hill, staring at the water and drinking rum all day, wondering what could have been. Adventure is in our blood. Freedom is in our blood. We can always get more treasure. Here is a chance to be free to roam the seas."

From the looks on their faces, I knew I had sold them.

"Aye. Nick's right. I'd have sores on my butt from sitting too long. Let's hide a bit of the loot on the ship, so if he is meaning to double-cross us, we still have something," Rhames conceded.

I continued while I still had their support. "We have to turn over most of it. There's a good chance he has someone watching us."

They nodded again. It was decided. At dawn we would pay a visit to the governor.

# CHAPTER EIGHT

### STEVEN BECKER
### THE WRECK OF THE *Ten Sail*

*E*ven though I had crossed the same water the day before, I was still wary of the bay. So I remained in the rigging keeping watch for coral heads and had Swift at the furthest point of the bowsprit with the lead. To my surprise, the soundings were all over four fathoms. We passed without incident, and early in the afternoon, we entered the harbor and dropped anchor, careful to select our mooring for a quick escape. As I looked at the mouth of the bay, though, I knew there was no real security. One ship could easily block the entrance to the bay and seal us inside.

My negotiations were more important now, and I rehearsed my offer as the men lashed the sails. The crew clearly shared my anxiety, because I heard Rhames remind the men to use quick-release knots and to prime and load the cannon.

Mason pulled the skiff towards the stern and tied it off while I, out of sight of prying eyes, slipped the boots over my feet. The salves Lucy had applied had helped and the cuts had started to heal, but it would be a few days before I could walk normally, or run if need be.

We had agreed that Mason, as the least pirate-looking and most level-headed of the bunch, would accompany me. Rory had fought to go with us, but I could not allow her to go into a potentially dangerous situation and I was still unsure of her motives. She and Lucy would remain hidden aboard. The hostage we had taken had likely given a full account of our ship and crew, but there was no point in flaunting that we had women aboard.

We climbed into the dinghy and sat at the bow while Rhames and Red each grabbed an oar and started pulling towards the pier. This was another calculated decision: to be rowed in like a captain. Gasparilla had taught me how to deal with power. He was well versed after his years in the Spanish court. In these negotiations, I knew I would need every bit of authority I could muster.

Two men, armed with cutlasses and pistols, met us at the pier. Ignoring the implied threat, we climbed the short ladder to the dock and followed the well-armed men to the governor's house.

From the corner of my eye, I saw Rhames and Red heading down a side street toward the stone house where I had been held. They were to make sure Blue was not captured, disable the cannons if possible, and reconnoiter the town.

The governor's house was a welcome relief from the hot day. The long eaves shaded the interior spaces from the sun and the large windows and open doors invited the sea breeze.

We were led to his office and, once inside, the two men took positions by the door as if to guard the exit. Bodden signaled Mason and me to sit, and we were again offered rum.

The governor pushed a document across the mahogany desk, and I moved closer. It was the letter of marque, the Holy Grail for any freebooter. I read the paper and saw that it was incomplete. There were no terms and the name of the captain and ship were blank. It was also unsigned—worthless. Bodden pulled the paper back and turned it around.

He was all business. The split was to be half each, a common agreement and one my crew had already decided was acceptable. We always had the option of hiding part of the booty, but a legal

## THE WRECK OF THE TEN SAIL

split was better than having the whole lot for yourself with nowhere to spend it. We waited while he filled in the information. It was all done except for the signing.

"Well, men, you are privateers for the king now." He paused, and I knew whatever surprise he had in store for us was about to be revealed. "Now, an honest partner would allow an inspection of his holds. Just so we know what's what."

This was unexpected. We had not talked about the possibility of a search, and it was not lost on me that the paper remained unsigned.

"I wouldn't want you to have to share what is already yours," he said.

Nor did I, but I weighed the value of the paper on his desk and decided to allow it. We had already agreed that in order to legitimize what we had, we would report taking the treasure, but be vague about its source. We had already resigned ourselves to losing half, knowing that what remained would be recorded and legal.

Besides, there were only two chests left from the original five, and the lone piece of silver cast as ballast in the bilge would likely remain undetected. The ballast had been a surprise and we had only discovered it when we'd brought it into the sunlight to use as a replacement anchor.

"Sign the paper and you can have your inspection," I said with more authority than I thought I could muster.

Bodden drank from his glass, paused, and drained the last inch in one sip. Then, taking his time, he dipped his pen in the inkwell, removed it with a flourish, and slowly placed the nib on the parchment.

The door flew open, and a small, hunched-over man entered the room. Startled, Bodden jumped, leaving a large blot on the page. I cursed. If not for all his ceremony, the letter would have been signed.

"This better be good, Pott." He looked hard at the man.

"Trouble at the pub," the man reported without raising his gaze from the floor.

The second the words were out of his mouth, I knew it could only be Rhames and Swift. They were the most belligerent of the crew. Being constantly on the run, I had been careful about rationing out our store of rum. I guessed the lure of the tavern and the delicious barmaid had been too much for them. I recalled the men playing dice in the corner and suspected this might be worse than a scuffle. Rhames was a notorious gambler, and a sore loser at that.

The governor got up and headed for the door. The document remained on his desk with a blob of ink where the signature should have been. Mason and I moved to follow until the governor spoke.

"Hold these men. Take them to the guardhouse until this is sorted out."

~

We were pushed inside the stone building, and the door slammed closed. I heard the bar placed on the outside and we waited for our eyes to adjust to the dim light of the small stone building. Not surprised, I saw Rhames and Swift sitting on the bench. Minutes before, I had envisioned myself sailing the Caribbean with a letter of marque, free to adventure and explore. Now we were imprisoned in a dim cell on one of the most neglected outposts in the Caribbean.

I glared at Rhames and Swift, but the pirates refused to meet my eyes.

"Care to explain?" I asked, keeping my voice low. I didn't want this discussion to be public.

"Bloody dice is what. We were cheated," Rhames complained.

I knew better than to ask why he was playing in the first place.

It was my fault for putting him in that position. "What's the result?" I asked, needing to know how bad it was.

"Damn near a hundred pounds," he said meekly.

I tried to process the amount, wondering how he could have lost so much so quickly. Many men never made that much in their lives.

"How?" I asked.

"We doubled down, hoping to get information. There weren't no sign of Blue and we thought we could pry a few tongues in the bar."

No sign of Blue was a good thing. As long as he remained at large, he was safe. As for the gambling debt, we could barter with some of the treasure. Maybe the letter of marque was still within reach.

I held that thought for all of a minute before footsteps approached and the door opened. I was temporarily blinded by the setting sun and it took a minute before I recognized Bodden's voice.

"Well, young captain, for all your fancy talk, it turns out that your lot is a bunch of pirates after all." The governor turned to the men behind him. "We'll string up these two and see if their captain can come up with the debt they owe. If not, we'll hang him and his mate as well."

Our situation had gone south in a matter of minutes, but I had no time to reflect on it. I had to save Rhames and Swift and get our crew to safety. "It's just a gambling debt," I argued. "Happens all the time. The men have been at sea for too long. We'll pay it off and be on our way."

"And I would do that why?" Bodden asked. "Maybe we ought to go have a look in your holds and see what you've really been up to."

My stomach sank. This was the worst case. He would surely loot the boat and hang us as pirates, enriching himself and increasing his name at the same time. I had to find a way out. Fortunately, there was a late-rising moon that night. It would be dark when we reached the ship, and I expected they would delay the search until the morning. I had several hours to remedy this, but had no idea how.

"Prisoners' rations for the lot," he spat before the door slammed, leaving us in the dark.

## CHAPTER NINE

STEVEN BECKER

### THE WRECK OF THE Ten Sail

*P*rison rations turned out to be better than I expected, mainly due to the mode of delivery. I didn't recognize her when she first entered the cell. The wide-brimmed hat covered much of her face. When she looked up and I saw her pale grey eyes, I almost forgot my circumstances.

"Stop staring and listen," she said.

I tried.

"Bodden's getting the gallows ready. I think he aims to hang the men in the morning. As for you, he'll ship you off to a more glamorous spot so more people can witness his capture of a famous pirate."

"I'm not even a pirate!" I felt like I was whining, and probably was.

She sat next to me on the bench. "By the time he finishes weaving the tale of your exploits, you will be."

The men were eating the turtle pie she had brought and were drinking from the cask of ale. At least they let men drink before they hung them.

"We'd pay you well to help us," I offered.

"It's too small an island. I'd be found out right away. Besides, Bodden's ready to search your ship. You'll be broke by the time the moon rises and the tide turns."

My hopes dimmed and I took a piece of the meat pie before it was gone. "Any way out, then?" I asked with my mouth full.

"I'd help if I could, but like I said, if they found out, they'd hang me and my father."

I heard a yelp from outside the door, followed by the sound of a body hitting the ground. Seconds later I heard another. Then Blue's head popped in the doorway. "We go now, Mr. Nick."

The men were already out the door, and I pulled on the boots to follow.

"Wait," she called to me.

I turned to look at the girl standing in the empty cell.

"You can't leave me. They'll think I had something to do with this."

I wanted no more blood on my hands. "Hurry, then. Come with us."

"Not without my father."

Every run-in I had with a woman made my life more complicated. Still, I couldn't leave her.

"We don't have time to get him."

"He can guide these waters as well as any man and help you find the treasure you were asking about," she said.

That changed things. If her father could do what she said, it would be worth the risk. Mason was a good navigator, but these waters required local knowledge, and that alone might be the difference between escape and death.

"You go to the ship and pull anchor. From the look of her, she's faster than any anchored in the bay. Their larger ships are on the ocean side. For them to stop you, they'd have to sail around the island, and they won't risk the east end at night. That same reef took the *Convent* and those other boats."

I was impressed with her knowledge. "Then where are we to meet?"

"There's a small sound to the east of the bay. Mind the points and stay in the channel. It's only a couple of miles across the land. We'll be there before you," she said before she left the guardhouse.

"Your name?" I called after her.

"Shayla," she answered and ran down the path.

I wasted no time. "Gather round," I whispered to the men.

We stood in a tight circle off to the side of the building. "Haul those guards into the cell and close the door. That way nothing will look amiss to a passerby. Blue, can you lead us to the ship?"

"We need the canoe, Mr. Nick. The pier is no good."

"Right, then. We follow Blue, then board the ship from the bay side. No matter what, we're getting out of here tonight."

The four of us grabbed the bodies and dragged them inside. I removed the darts from the men's necks. Let them wonder what mysteries killed these men. The last thought I had before closing the door was that we were pirates again, but our other option was certain death. We followed Blue into the brush, fighting against the sharp palmetto leaves and small cacti as we went. My feet hurt inside the boots, but it would have been worse without them.

Suddenly, when we were no more than ten feet into the brush, Blue stopped and held his hand for quiet.

"Someone run the other way."

At first, I thought he meant the girl, but he knew she had gone and would recognize her light footfall. "A man?" I asked.

"There must have been three of them," Rhames said. "Little bugger missed one."

I doubted Blue had misjudged the situation, but nevertheless we had been discovered. "Better move, then," I concluded.

We ran through the brush, now careless about the noise we made and certain an alarm had been sounded. The brush thinned suddenly and we found ourselves in an open pasture. The cuts on my feet were chafing against the leather of the boots, and I knew I was holding the group back. "Blue. How far to the canoe?" I called ahead, wincing from the pain.

"Not far, Mr. Nick."

"Go on. I'll find it and come in the second load."

I saw him confer with Rhames and Swift, who ran back for me. They hoisted me between them and I draped one arm over each of their shoulders. Like the three-legged races I remembered from my childhood, we made our way across the pasture and found the bay. Blue and Mason ran to the water and started to remove the palm fronds from the canoe.

The narrow craft was made for two, so it rode low in the water with Rhames, Swift, Mason, and me in it. Blue stayed in the water, clinging to the stern as Rhames and Swift took the first shift with the paddles. With the extra weight, we had little freeboard and I feared even the smallest wave would swamp the boat. Thankfully the moon had not yet risen and there was no wind. With a bit of luck, we would blend into the night and make it back to the ship.

An hour later the lights from the town came into view. We closed on the *Panther,* but as we did, we noticed a number of lights aboard. We were too late.

"Slow down and paddle to shore," I called to Rhames.

Rhames turned and gave me a questioning look.

"Bastard governor's gone for the treasure," Swift muttered.

Near shore, I jumped out to beach the boat. There was nothing the four of us could do now. With no arms between us, save Blue's blowgun, we would have to wait them out. We sat on the jagged rocks for what seemed like hours before the last light moved down the ladder and onto a waiting boat. The jovial voices of the men, fresh from looting our ship, carried across the bay.

Disheartened, we piled back in the canoe. We paddled straight out into the bay on a course that would take us out of sight of the settlement. Lanterns were visible along the coastline and I guessed they were searching for us on shore. I assumed they didn't know about the canoe. Regardless, we were careful to make a wide loop before approaching the ship. If we were seen boarding the ship after killing two of their men, they would surely fire on us.

By the time we turned to the ship, the moon was in the sky and the light it cast showed the land toward the northeast. I picked out the two points where Shayla and her father were to wait for us and wondered if they would make our rendezvous.

With the *Panther*'s hull now screening us from the settlement, we changed course and headed directly for the ship. Slowly, we slid next to her. Although the tide was in our favor for the moment, it would make our escape that much harder. With only a light wind, we needed the assistance of the outgoing tide to exit the bay. I willed the moon higher in the sky, knowing when it hit its apex the tide would be at its peak and start flowing outward. But it had only been up for an hour, leaving half the night before it could aid us.

As we brushed the hull of the ship, we called up to the deck, hoping the governor had not taken the crew as well. Finally Lucy's head appeared over the rail.

"Drop us a ladder," I called up to her.

Minutes later we were on deck and I assessed the damage.

Red confirmed that the treasure was indeed gone. Keeping my composure, I tried to reassure them.

"Nothing you could do," I said.

Red and Lucy stood silently with their heads down. That's when I noticed what else was missing.

"Where's Rory?"

"Strange thing about her," Red said. "She showed them straight away where the treasure was, and then asked that they take her to see the governor."

## CHAPTER TEN

### STEVEN BECKER

### THE WRECK OF THE Ten Sail

"There's nothing to be gained staying here. That bastard governor will arrest us at first light and either take the ship or burn her," Rhames said.

I was hesitating, wanting to be certain of Rory's intentions. If she had a plan to help us, I needed to know, but there had been no indication of that and I was faced with the uncomfortable reality that Rory's actions were treachery, plain and simple, that I had been played the fool.

"Right, then," I said with more confidence than I felt. "Might as well get a jump on the tide and pull the ship." I turned my head to feel the direction of the wind, hoping it would allow us to sail out of the bay against the tide, but I barely noticed any. "Maybe it'll freshen with the sunrise. If we can reach the mouth of the bay by then, we can catch it."

"There's a couple of small islands not a day's sail from here," Mason said. "If we get out of here, we can head towards one and regroup."

I looked at the chart spread out on the navigation table. It would have been more comfortable in the cabin with a lantern, but we didn't want the light to alert anyone watching from shore that we were preparing to slip from the harbor. Let them keep thinking the handful of folk they left aboard were half-drunk and waiting for the rest of their crew.

"I'll take first turn on the oars," I said and went to the ladder. Really, I wanted to get some time alone to think about our situation and get out of the judging gaze of the men. Rhames took the wheel and Swift and Red went forward to retrieve the anchor. Blue and Lucy had already gone below to make more darts for their blowguns.

"I'll give a hand," Mason said and climbed down the ladder behind me.

Of the crew, my only sure ally right now was Mason. We sat next to each other on the bench seat and started gently rowing towards the stern to catch the hawser that Swift was waiting to toss. It hit the deck of the small boat and Mason tied a bridle to two belay pins attached to the skiff.

We waited in silence while they raised the anchor. I winced as the links of the chain rattled through the opening in the bow, loud enough to attract attention if anyone was listening. I took the chance of a slight delay and called for them to slow down. Anxiously, I watched the shoreline for any sign that our escape had been noticed, but there was no action, nor any movement from the boats in the harbor. Finally the anchor left the water and was secured by the two men.

We were drifting with the tide now, its movement taking us in the wrong direction—toward the pier. With a sense of urgency, Mason and I took to the oars and pulled with everything we had. The initial effort required to get the boat moving against the flow of water was backbreaking, but once done, although we were not moving fast, the hull slid silently through the water at what I guessed was about a knot. It would be hours of grueling work, but once the tide turned we would easily be in a position to raise sail and escape through the bay's entrance, though the lack of wind was still troubling.

"What about those natives?" Mason asked as we settled into a rhythm.

I had not forgotten about Shayla and her father. "Don't guess there's much we can do for them having to tow the boat and all." In truth, I had little interest in them. I was still smarting from Rory's possible betrayal and wanted nothing to do with another woman.

"Send Blue in the canoe," he suggested. "We could use their knowledge if we return."

I knew at least I would be back for the treasure, if not to find out where Rory stood, and it was true we would need help, but I was curious about Mason's interest. As he had joined the crew later, he was not vested in the treasure we had lost. Only the silver ballast was his, and right now he was wealthier than the lot of us combined.

"What is it about that wreck that you would risk everything to come back for it?"

"There you have me," he said. "Rumor is that the single silver ballast in the hold is part of a large batch cast by the English governor in Jamaica to trick pirates and privateers. With the king's son aboard one of those boats, there would surely be treasure as well. But thirty years ago, the English were at war with France, and the Spanish who still ruled these waters would plunder any foreign ship they came across. You'd want to hide your riches if you were them, and the story goes they had it cast into ballast and hidden in the keel."

"But the old man said the wreck was deeper than they could dive."

"It is, but there's something else he didn't tell you. They found and searched the *Convent*, which led the convoy, but she was just a military ship. It was the *Ludlow* carrying the ballast that was never found."

Now I understood his interest, but how could it help us, and how could we reach it? Regardless, it would be worth having a guide and supplementing our skeleton crew with two more bodies, if nothing else. If Blue was willing to search for them, there was no harm in taking on the two passengers.

"Rhames," I called to the ship, less cautious than before. We were now at least a mile from the harbor, and I had looked back several times and seen no sign of pursuit. And why would they? They had our treasure... and Rory.

"Yo," he called back from the forepeak.

"Get Blue into the canoe. We're going to see if we can find the old man and his daughter. He could come in handy as a pilot." I wasn't exactly lying.

"Aye. We could use a set of eyes that knows what's what."

A few minutes later I heard the sound of the canoe moving towards us. The sleek craft quickly pulled alongside and I saw Lucy was with Blue.

"Be faster with two, and I'm not leaving him to run off with no local," she said before I could ask.

I nodded. The canoe could take the weight. "You know where to look for them?" I asked Blue.

"We'll find them," he answered and they paddled silently away. There was no doubt he would find them. We watched them disappear into the darkness, then I called back to Rhames to spell us. He sent Swift and Red and we exchanged places.

Back at the wheel, I wondered if the rumors about the wreck and its fortune in silver were true. Without the treasure in our hold, we were no longer worth much to anyone. Perhaps it was worth risking a return to the island.

There were few ways to come across treasure in the Caribbean, and *treasure hunter* sounded a lot better than *wrecker*, those sketchy characters that worked up and down the Florida coast and the Bahamas looking for ships in distress, sometimes even luring them onto the reefs.

But how could we reach riches too deep to free-dive for?

Mason joined me a few minutes later and I began questioning him about the procedure.

"It's all new," he said excitedly. "A helmet of sorts that has a faceplate you can see through, with a hose run from a pump on the deck of a boat."

I had to admit I was entranced.

"I saw a piece in a newspaper a while back," he continued, "about two brothers on the continent who fashioned one to allow firefighters to enter burning buildings."

"Where would we get something like this?" I asked, dreaming about the possibility of breathing underwater and finding treasure. Suddenly, it wasn't just this one wreck I was interested in, but the hundreds of ships laden with gold that had gone down in these waters over the centuries.

He thought for a few minutes. "Havana would be the most likely place to find what we need. It's only two days' sail."

I wasn't sure it would work, but it wasn't as though we had another plan. Besides, an idea was forming in my head. The salvage operation could give us the ideal cover to get back to Grand Cayman.

I felt the boat pick up speed. The moon was on its way back to the horizon, and the tide had turned. Keeping an eye out for Blue and Lucy, I called for the skiff to return to the *Panther*.

## CHAPTER ELEVEN

### STEVEN BECKER
### THE WRECK OF THE Ten Sail

High in the rigging, I strained to see through the predawn glow, scanning the horizon for the canoe with Blue, Lucy, and, if we were lucky, the two locals. We were near the north end of the sound and just a mile from the ocean. There was no sign of them and I was getting worried.

There was still little wind but I could see ripples on the water. I felt a small puff every few minutes that indicated there might be a change with the dawn. Blue and Lucy were somewhere to the east and I needed to spot them quickly before the rising sun blinded me. The first rays were already peeking above the horizon. Squinting into the light, I could just make out something moving near the mouth of the sound. It was a canoe riding low in the water.

"There they are!"

I saw Mason shield his eyes and then noticed the look on his face. When I looked at the canoe again, I understood his concern. With our drift and their position, we would be past them before they could reach us.

Another puff caught me off guard, further convincing me that the wind would be up soon, and blowing from the southeast—perfect for our destination. But the fresh breeze and the friendly tide worked against any hope we had in recovering the canoe. Mason changed course to move us out of the main current, drifting as close to the edge of the sound as he dared without knowledge of the water. He had Swift drop the lead and call soundings from the bow. We were in less than two fathoms of water, as shallow as we dared.

The boat was still moving too fast.

I jumped from the rigging, ran to the hold, and slid down the ladder. I rifled through the locker until I found a spare foresail, then, with the canvas under my arm, I made for the deck and called Rhames and Red over.

"Fashion a sea anchor," I said as I crossed the deck in the direction of the cabin. Inside the galley, I found the fishing line we had used a few days earlier. It would serve. I took both spools to the stern rail, shooting a quick glance back at the men tying bowline knots to the sail. They clearly understood what I wanted.

A proper buoy would have been better suited for what I had in mind, but I had nothing other than a rope fender. Untying it from the rail and attaching it to the end of the fishing line, I tossed the fender over the stern and paid out the line. Just before the first spool was about to run out, I wound several loops around my arm, tied the bitter end to the next spool, and paid out that line as well. The second line was nearing its end now, and I glanced up at the fender now floating several hundred feet behind the boat.

I tied the line off and helped the men drop the drogue into the water. The force of the wake threatened to yank the canvas from our arms, but we held on until our progress slowed enough to tie off the lines.

I was able to see the sail had done its part to slow the ship, but from the speed and angle the canoe was traveling, I knew they would fall behind us. I had to signal Blue that the fender was behind the boat.

## THE WRECK OF THE TEN SAIL

I went below, grabbed a small piece of mirror from the cabin, and climbed back into the rigging. I caught the sun on its surface and reflected the light toward the canoe. With no prearranged signal, I did my best to catch their attention, then I moved the light from the stern to the fender. There was nothing to do now but hope they understood.

I climbed back down and took a position near the starboard rail. With the speed of our ship slowed and the current working in their favor, they were making good progress, but they were still going to miss us. The buoy line was our last chance. I went to the stern as they approached, now close enough to see the distressed look on their faces as they realized their predicament. The two men were paddling for all they were worth and I thought for a second they might have a chance, but the stretch of water between us seemed to be growing.

"The fender. There's a line tied to it!" I yelled, but I knew they didn't understand. "Paddle harder," I yelled, trying to encourage them.

Blue threw up his hands, but just as I was about to give up, I saw Lucy point to the fender and yell at the men. The women were dog-paddling, aiding the men. It was going to be close.

"Raise the mains," I heard Mason yell at the men.

"We'll lose them for sure," I pleaded. "We can't."

"Just watch."

Swift and Red climbed the main mast and unfurled the sail. Rhames untied the slack line from a pin on the rail and wound it around a block. The sail rose as he pulled. It fluttered, and for a brief minute before it caught the wind, the boat stalled. I looked back at the canoe, at the four all paddling frantically towards the line. I held my breath. If the sail caught before they reached the line, it would be pulled away from them. I could only hope Mason was right.

Another puff caught the sail, and it fluttered again, stalling us more, but we had only seconds before the ship would react and increase her speed. I ran back to the stern just in time to see Blue reach into the water and grab the fender.

Now I had to hope the thin line would hold while he pulled them towards us. But Blue was careful and pulled slowly and evenly, minimizing the stress to the line until they were within a rope's throw from the ship. I tossed a cable to the old man in the bow. He caught it and tied it off before the four collapsed in exhaustion.

The mouth of the bay was close and we had little time to secure the canoe and get the group aboard before we hit open water. I pulled at the cable, then called down to Blue to draw the canoe close enough to the hull to reach the ladder. The wind was up now, blowing at ten knots, and though it would benefit us once we were out of the bay, I cursed it for impeding our effort. As the canoe approached the stern of the boat, the water churned where the outgoing tide from the bay met the ocean. The proximity of the boats was now dangerous. One wave could pitch the *Panther* forward, raising the stern enough to crush the canoe and all those in it. We would have to act quickly.

The chop increased, but Lucy managed to grab hold of the ladder and help the old man and his daughter to climb ahead of her. Last up the ladder was Blue, and finally all four were aboard.

Before we could exchange greetings, the old man left us and went to Mason, pointing at what I could only assume was an unseen obstacle in the water ahead. Reacting quickly, Mason made the appropriate course correction. It might have saved us to have rescued the old man after all.

We were now on the verge of entering the darker open water. There was no time to bring the canoe aboard, so I released enough line to allow it to coast on a wave behind us and called for help to retrieve the sea anchor. Blue assisted me as we released the first two lines and let the water spill from the home-made drogue before hauling the sail in.

Without the additional drag, the *Panther* rose in the water, and soon we were in blue water under full sail. I dropped to the deck. It wasn't an hour past dawn and I was exhausted.

Shayla, standing at the starboard rail, gave me a weak smile, looking equally taxed. But before I could respond, I saw Rhames, Swift, and Red coming towards me. This was the pirate faction, and I knew I had wronged them with the decisions I had made on behalf of the group. It appeared there was one more battle to fight before I could rest. Reluctantly, I rose to my feet and met them amidships.

Rhames spoke for the group. "We need to talk."

He had always been my ally and had helped me gain control of our small band after the Navy had sunk the *Floridablanca*. I hoped this was more for show than real dissension.

"You know our way," he started. "We decides together where we're headed and what we're to do there."

I nodded. This was the democracy of a pirate crew. The captain was voted and served at the whim of his men, having sole authority only under arms.

"There was no time," I pleaded.

"We knows, and it was me who started some of the trouble with the dice, but we need to agree now on a plan."

He had let me off the hook by taking ownership of the trouble his gambling had caused, but I still needed them to come around to my plans. I thought back to Gasparilla, suddenly wishing I had his savvy for manipulating a crew. But there was no need. There was no aggression visible on their faces. Red and Swift only stood quietly while Rhames waited for my response. I decided on honesty.

"I aim to get the treasure back," I said.

## CHAPTER TWELVE

*I* knew from the look on the men's faces they had their doubts.

"And how do you propose to do that?" Rhames asked. "It's all fine and good, but the governor and that red-headed witch you're so fond of aren't likely to let us walk in and take it. Maybe you can get my hundred pounds back from those crooks with the loaded dice while you're at it."

Red and Swift nodded in agreement.

The tide had turned against me and I thought for a second, trying to play it calm while I searched frantically for an idea. "We give him something he wants more," I said. It sounded good, but I had no idea what that might be.

"Give him more treasure," Mason said from the helm.

"This isn't your concern," Red returned over his shoulder.

"Give him a say," I said. "He's proven himself to be a full member of the crew." I had been meaning to have Mason voted a full share and this seemed to be a good time. "I say he's got a full stake."

The three men talked amongst themselves for a minute and

agreed. This evened the odds slightly, but if push came to shove, I was still outvoted three to two.

"What are you speaking of?" Rhames asked, turning the crew's attention to Mason.

"The Wreck of the Ten Sail; that's what we offer him. There's a rumor that one of the ships went down with a ton of silver in its hold. The islanders saved most of the men, but the silver was never recovered. That man, Phillip," Mason said, gesturing to the old man now standing at the bow with his daughter, "he says he was one of the men that loaded it in Port Royal."

Rhames was unimpressed.

"There's enough booty spread on the bottom of the sea for every man she's claimed to spend in hell," he said. "What's so bloody important about this lot?"

"If Bodden is as corrupt as most," I said, "he's waiting out his term here, cursing the sun and heat and accumulating as much money as he can to retire when the Crown calls him home. They're all the same. That Spanish haul he took from us is too easy to identify and would need to be brokered if he wants to skim some for himself. King George would have his head if he found out." I paused to let this sink in.

"So what?" Red asked.

"So we parlay," I responded.

All eyes were on me now and a plan started to form in my head. Hopefully it would make sense when it came out of my mouth. "We offer him the silver in exchange for the treasure. That he can hoard and spend. It'll cost him a bit to recast it, but it won't have the taint of pirates."

"And how are you going to trust him?" Rhames asked.

"We just need to stay valuable enough to him that he has no choice but to remain trustworthy."

The three smirked at that and, content for the moment, returned to their duties, Swift replacing Mason at the wheel.

"You almost lost them there," Mason said when we were alone.

He was right. Pirate law is a fickle thing. What I needed was enough money to buy my own ship, or buy them out of this one. Maybe a partnership with Mason was in the cards when this was over.

We were beating into the wind, working our way around the east end of the island. I planned to anchor off Bodden Town on the ocean side this time. It was a better mooring in case we needed a quick escape.

All hands were on the starboard rail as we cleared the point of the east end and looked on the breakers marking the Wreck of the Ten Sail. There was nothing visible. Over the thirty years, the rough seas had destroyed anything above the waterline. With the wind at our back, our speed picked up and I gathered the men to explain my plan to ensure our safety.

Our four main guns were thirty-five-pound carronades, but we had no proper ammunition. Still, Rhames and I moved one of the starboard guns over to the port side, and I sent Swift and Red into the hold for anything we could fire. A pile of chain and rocks soon appeared on deck.

I was betting the prevailing winds would remain and allow us to anchor with our starboard side to land. "Bring up some cotton as well," I called. "There'll be a lot of windage shooting this lot."

None of the projectiles were the proper size, meaning unwanted gaps between the barrel and the round, but we were in need of any advantage that could be gained with only four guns. After some final adjustments, I felt better about our defenses.

Although it would be dangerous, I sought to reach the harbor under the cover of darkness, giving us the advantage of surprise and the opportunity to choose our anchorage and adjust our defenses. But now, it was only noon and we had hours to kill.

"Someone go below and ask the man where we can get fresh water. We could use his help to navigate as well."

We anchored a safe distance from the coast several miles from the town. Rhames led an excursion for meat, returning with two turtles that we quartered and set out to dry. Fresh water wasn't as easy to come by. There was no easy source on the island. Blue had reported as much after his reconnaissance the day we arrived, and Phillip confirmed his assessment. Every drop of drinking water on Grand Cayman came from the sky, which was now a vibrant blue, without a cloud in sight. Another month and we would be in the rainy season, but for now we would have to keep an eye on our supply.

It was getting dark. We pulled anchor and made for Bodden Town. Less than an hour later, with Mason at the wheel and the men in the rigging, we coasted past the last ship in the anchorage. I wanted to be to the west, in order to benefit from the trade winds if a quick departure was needed. With a plan this thin, I suspected it might be. We were running dark, and orders were whispered so as not to alert the other ships, though many looked empty. Swift called out six fathoms from the bow and I gave a hand signal to the men in the rigging to drop sail. Slowly, without the benefit of canvas, we coasted to a crawl, and I went forward to inspect our anchorage.

A foot at a time, the ink-black water swallowed the anchor chain as Swift and I eased it out. Finally, when my hands were raw from the rusty iron links, it hit bottom and the ship stopped and swung. I gave orders to prepare her for both battle and escape, just in case things went badly while I was ashore.

~

Mason and I were rowed to the beach at dawn. It was my intention to see the governor before he had time to prepare. Of course, there was a good chance he already knew we were here, but we had heard no alarms during the night to indicate anyone had spied our entry to the harbor.

"Wait here," I told the men as we waded ashore.

The streets were deserted and we reached the governor's house without incident. It felt odd walking to his door after everything that had occurred, but here we were. If I was to keep control of the ship and her crew, I needed a deal. I breathed in and knocked on the hardwood.

The surprised look on the servant's face when he let us in told me my plan had worked. Mason and I were shown to the foyer and told to wait. A long quarter of an hour later, the governor appeared, still dressed in his bed robe.

"Look what we have here," he said. "I wasn't expecting company for breakfast." He gave an order to the servant waiting nearby to set a place for us and we followed him into the dining room.

I was startled to see Rory when I entered. She was dressed in finery and merely nodded to us as if we were acquaintances. A pit formed in my stomach.

Bodden laughed at my obvious surprise. "I'll spare the introductions," he said as he sat at the head of the table.

I started to open my mouth to plead our case, but he put a finger to his lips and waved for the food to be brought in. It was clear he intended to extend my agony.

For me, eating seemed impossible, and when I wasn't under the watchful gaze of the governor, I stole glances at Rory. She continued ignoring me, smiling at the governor as she played at being the lady. I still held out hope that she would help us and that this was a ruse for the governor's benefit.

Despite my weak appetite, I managed to finish my meal, as did Mason. Bodden on the other hand took his time. Finally, when I could stand it no longer, he wiped his mouth with his sleeve and addressed us.

"I'm thinking you have a proposal to present," he said.

I glanced at Rory, but she was looking down.

"You know why we're here," I said.

"I do. But…" He put out his hands and shrugged. "Why don't you amuse me?"

"We have come for our treasure," I started. "We have something to exchange for it." He nodded for me to continue. "We intend to mount an operation to retrieve silver from one of the ships lost in the wreck on the east end."

"Ah, the Ten Sail," he said and sat straighter in his chair.

I knew I had his attention now. "The treasure you stole from us is of little value to you personally. The silver, though, would make you a wealthy man."

The governor leaned forward. "Go on."

"We will trade equal weights of the silver for the treasure… and the girl." I threw out the last bit to gauge her reaction. There was none.

Bodden laughed. "The girl can make up her own mind when this affair is settled. Go ahead, boy, see if the seas will yield your dreams."

## CHAPTER THIRTEEN

STEVEN BECKER
THE WRECK OF THE
*Ten Sail*

With the seas on our starboard quarter and our sails on a beam reach, the wind remained brisk, and soon the island blended into the horizon. Something had finally gone right and there was no sign of pursuit. I slept the rest of the day and was shaken awake around midnight to take the second watch.

"Come on, you can't sleep all night." Rhames prodded me again.

Despite my body's objections, I rose and went to the helm to relieve Mason, who gave me our course. With no hazards near, and the wind behaving, I lashed the wheel and went below. Mason, Rhames, and I sat around the table in the galley with the chart spread out in front of us.

"I'm figuring we're here," Mason said, pointing a stubby finger at the chart at a point halfway through the passage from Grand Cayman to Cuba.

"Where do you expect to make landfall?" I asked.

He pointed to a bay near the western tip of the island. "We'll be safe there," he said. "Pirates'll be in the south end, and the Spanish fleet will be in Havana. Nothing to worry about on the east end, just sugarcane plantations."

I had a working knowledge of the currents and knew he was right. The Gulf Stream curved around the western end of the island before it followed the northern coast to the east. "So, we go on foot to Havana?"

"Reckon that's the safest way," Mason said.

Rhames frowned. "That looks like a week's walk there and back."

"We'll need horses," I said.

His frown deepened, but I'd already decided to leave him on the ship. Mason and I would go with Blue. We might not blend in, but we didn't look like pirates. Mason was about to roll up the chart when the old man emerged from the companionway.

"You might want to reconsider," he said.

"And how's that, Phillip?" I asked suspiciously.

Phillip had helped us clear the coral heads blocking the bay at Grand Cayman, but to me he was still an unknown. I had no idea about the extent of his travels.

"I've been around these waters a few times. I was born in Port Royal after my father, a seafaring man from England, escaped there after freeing my mum from slavery in Jamaica. With mixed blood I had limited options, so I signed on with a merchant ship. Gave up my sea legs when the ship wrecked in the Ten Sail," he said.

"What would your course be?" I asked.

"To cross by land from the south is a bit tricky. I wouldn't say it's a regular mountain range, but I wouldn't want to take that route. There's an anchorage on the northern coast that'd save you days of travel."

Rhames snorted. "Less time we're there the better. If it wasn't for the Spanish fleet, I'd sail right into Havana."

We laughed at his bravado.

Our course decided, I left for the helm to take the dog watch. Before I climbed the ladder, I turned to Phillip.

"Is your daughter settling in all right?" I asked him. "I haven't seen her since you came aboard."

"I'd be fine," Shayla said, coming up behind me. She was just out of one of the cabins and rubbing sleep from her eyes.

She was stunning, even in this state, her ivory skin a stark contrast to the dark mahogany fittings of the cabin. I nodded to her cordially, trying to ignore her beauty, and headed above deck. Even though, by all appearances, Rory had turned on us, the feisty Englishwoman still weighed heavily on my mind.

I stood at the helm trying to sort through all that had happened when I heard someone approach.

"Ya mind a bit of company?" Shayla asked. She'd followed me.

I turned to her. Her beauty unsettled me. I decided to distract myself by pressing her for information.

"Back at the pub. Why did you help me?" I asked.

"It was good to see someone take an interest in my father. Too many back there think he's crazy with his talk of treasure."

Her explanation seemed sound, but I wanted more. "Tell me about him."

"You and your lot put the sparkle back in his eye," she explained before turning and gazing out to sea.

"Is he who he says he is?" I wanted the words back as soon as they left my mouth. "Sorry, that was badly put."

"I hear what you're asking." She tilted her head back. "If you're to rely on his advice, you ought to know if it's good."

I looked at her skin glowing in the moonlight and I almost lost my train of thought. This was one of those moments where it was better not to talk. I concentrated on steering the next wave and waited for her to continue.

"He tells it true. He's been landlocked since the wreck in '94. The Wreck of the Ten Sail. He's not had the desire for the sea since."

"But he seems anxious to talk about the treasure," I responded, pressing her further. Like all other women I had dealings with, Shayla's words were like a spell. They seemed woven especially to confuse me.

"Rumors always floated around that he knew something about some mysterious hidden treasure. Ballast stones cast from silver, they say. Most thought he was crazy, but not all. That's why Bodden kept him close. He set him up with the pub and gave us a way to earn a living so he could keep an eye on him. And..." Her words trailed off as she looked out to sea. "Bodden's a greedy bastard," she added.

I agreed with her about the governor. "So why trust us?"

"Some have ridiculed him, others called him an outright liar. Men have come and gone over the years, but none truly believed him, at least not enough to spend the time and gold it would take to raise the treasure."

She pointed to two porpoises following our wake and went to the rail to watch them. Her dress, if you could call it that, was translucent in the moonlight and I could see every curve of her body.

She turned back to me. "You're the first that understood it was real. Somehow my father sensed this about you."

"What about Bodden?"

"Bodden," she said in a tone I hadn't heard from her before. "Bodden always gets what he wants. He thinks because he set us up, that we owe him, if you know what I mean." She looked away.

I was silent for a second, confused by what she said. She turned back to me and her look told the tale.

"'Twas only a few times, but I'm glad to be free of it," she said and moved back to my side.

I tried to ignore her closeness by asking more questions. Clearly she was not going away, and I looked up at the moon to guess how much time remained until my watch ended. We talked about this and that, anything to lighten the mood after the revelation about her and the governor. I wondered if Rory was in the same predicament.

Finally, Red came up and took the helm. After briefing him on our course and taking a last breath of fresh air, I nodded goodnight to the girl and went below.

I thought she had remained on deck, but just as I was about to close the door to my cabin, she slid through the gap. I almost asked what she was doing, but the words never made it out of my mouth.

In the glow of the moonlight I watched her pull the shift over her head, and there she was, standing naked in front of me. Again, I didn't trust my voice. I was not inexperienced in these matters, but I had never been with a woman by her free will. That unnerved me.

Before I could react, she came to me and the heat and passion of youth took over.

## CHAPTER FOURTEEN

### STEVEN BECKER

# THE WRECK OF THE *Ten Sail*

*I* awoke with the dawn when I heard the call of 'land ho'. As I heard the men beating to quarters, I unwound myself from Shayla, immediately regretting our passion. Like the rising sun, Rory had come blazing back into my thoughts. For whatever reason, I still believed her to be true. A hard knock on the cabin door forced my remorse aside. I dressed and went on deck.

Phillip and Mason were both at the helm and I couldn't shake the look that passed between them as I approached. I did my best to ignore it, hoping the girl would give me a reprieve and remain below. Without comment, I took the spyglass and pointed it toward the point of land on our port side. The sea broke about fifty feet from shore, indicating a reef. I checked our course. We were a bit close for my liking, but when I looked over at Mason, I saw he was turning the wheel to allow us more leeway.

The entire crew was on deck now, gathered at the rail, watching the passing land. We rounded the point and turned west, sailing a safe distance from the shore. We were on a run of close to six knots, I reckoned. The *Panther* had gained a few knots after the work we had done on the hull.

An hour later, Phillip pointed to a protected bay and directed Mason into its opening—a perfect anchorage, except for the ship already there. From the stench of her, I knew her to be a slaver. There was no amount of lye that could rid a ship of the smell of misery and death. We were the same size and in better condition, so I doubted they would have any interest in trying us. Likely, they were there to raid—an act of desperation this close to Havana. Still, we anchored to port and reloaded the carronade facing the slaver, just in case.

The old man was right. It was a good anchorage, a small bay with deep water and a small river running into it from the far end where we could replenish our water supply. I gathered the crew and gave orders before Rhames rowed Mason and me to shore. As we passed the slaver, a chill ran through my spine.

It was strange how different the land here was for being only two days' sail away from Grand Cayman. From the ship I had seen the hills, peaks reaching into the low clouds and descending into green cane fields. Thankfully, there was little sign of the sharp, jagged rocks that had cut me on Cayman.

We found a well-traveled path just beyond the beach and headed west towards Havana. Large sugarcane plantations were on our left, the green stalks stretching as far as we could see. After a few miles, the path became more of a road. We walked in silence, to prevent drawing attention—a smart choice, as most of our talk would have been of treasure. Lucy had wrapped my feet again before our journey, but now they were chafing against the boots.

"What do you figure a horse goes for?" I asked. From the chart it looked like we had to cover sixty miles to reach the city. Besides my feet, I didn't want to lose a week traveling there and back.

"We've got enough silver. Maybe we can make a deal on a loan from one of these plantations," Mason said.

We walked another few miles, until a cart path intersected the road. A quarter mile in, I could see a large house. "Let's give it a try."

An hour later we were a few pieces of silver lighter, but covering twice the ground. The horses were old and came with a stern warning to be easy on them, but it was better than walking—that was, until my bottom began to hurt. I had never ridden before and was soon feeling muscles I didn't know I had. Mason had said it took some time to get used to, but after a few hours I was done for the day.

"It's almost dark. Why don't we find a place to make camp?" I said.

Blue, who had been trotting a little ahead of us, turned back. "I find a spot."

He increased his pace, amazing me with his energy. Mason and I dismounted and led the two worn-out horses to a pool of rainwater. We waited until they drank their fill, then moved away before the mosquitoes showed up. Blue was back quickly and led us to a protected clearing off the road. The site had been used, and there was a fire pit, but we decided to forgo a fire so we could remain concealed.

We sat quietly eating dried turtle meat and some bananas that Blue had foraged. I tried to relax, but the two women were still competing for time in my head. I needed to stop the chatter. I did the only thing I could think of and asked Mason about the treasure.

"It's there, all right. I spent an hour or so talking to Phillip last night. He was on the ship that carried it. We went into the hold and I showed him the ballast. He confirmed that it was one and the same. Damn clever way to move wealth."

I had to agree, and it made sense. Gasparilla had told me about the privateers. Legal pirates commissioned by countries on the continent, allowed to roam freely, enrich themselves and their benefactors at the expense of the merchant trade. In the last years of the eighteenth century, the Caribbean had been a free-for-all.

"Phillip told me that over fifty ships left Port Royal in the group that wrecked in the Caymans," Mason continued. "But the convoys often got split up by weather, leaving them easy prey for the rogues prowling the sea. As a safeguard, the British began casting their wealth into common objects for transport, hoping they might be overlooked in a raid."

"Did all the ships do this?" I asked.

"Not all. But the *Ludlow* certainly did, and the old man knows where she is. Unfortunately, she's too deep to free-dive. A trained man might reach sixty feet, but he wouldn't have the ability to explore. And the silver's in the bilge."

"So how do we get the treasure?" I asked.

"Only way I reckon we can explore is to use the headgear I told you about. That way you can be supplied by air from a pump on the surface."

"So, no one's ever done it?" I asked, suddenly alarmed that we had taken such a gamble to come here, and now relied on a method that was mostly untested. Despite the uncertainty I was still intrigued. "You know what we need, then?" I was trusting Mason more than I probably should have. I had to admit, part of me was excited by the venture.

"Got a list in my head. Shouldn't be too much. Some leather, hose, a bit of glass and some hardware." He paused. "And a pump."

That shouldn't be too hard to find, I thought and realized we would need a cart to carry it all back. I was suddenly glad for the horses, even though I still felt the soreness in my privates. As tired as I was, sleep eluded me. My thoughts wavered between the two women and the treasure. I tried to find a comfortable position to rest and put all of it out of my mind.

We spent the night on the ground in the clearing and set off at dawn, following the same road. It was dull traveling overland, passing nothing but acre after acre of sugarcane, but, by nightfall of the second day, Mason said we were less than a day away. I slept better that night, my body now accustomed to the horses and my feet almost totally healed. I was excited to see Havana. It would be the first real city I had seen in over five years.

⁓

*I* knew we were getting close. People of all kinds were on the road now, some walking, others riding. Several large carriages passed by, their occupants concealed behind curtains. Finally, near dusk, we reached the city, but Mason thought it better to wait and camp one more night. He knew the dangers of an unknown city after dark and, despite my eagerness, I succumbed to his wisdom. We were eating the last of our turtle and making plans for the next day, when Blue appeared.

Not comfortable with horses, he had traveled by foot, the mode of transport more suitable for the pygmy. But now he was more agitated than I had seen him before.

"It is bad here, Mr. Nick. Many people give the evil eye."

"We are only traders here, Blue. No one knows our purpose."

"They know Englishmen have money to spend. But Blue will watch them."

"Thank you. We should take turns on watch tonight," I said to Mason. He agreed.

It was another sleepless night for me. Although we were not in the city itself, we were close enough to smell it, and there was traffic coming and going late into the night.

I felt like I had just fallen asleep when Mason woke me. It was about an hour after dawn and the road was already choked with merchants bringing all manner of goods and livestock into the city. We fell in behind one group, walking our horses and trying to blend in. Blue had disappeared again, but I knew he was watching.

After all the waiting, I had to admit I was disappointed. Havana had a unique waterfront with old forts and buildings, but the market was smelly and crowded with people pushing and arguing in Spanish, of which I knew few words. The streets were narrow, their ruts full of muck. Reluctantly, we found a stable and paid the owner a few bits of silver to feed and water our horses, then set off on foot.

It was a simple matter finding the goods Mason needed, although, looking at the pile in the cart, I had no idea how it would all go together. Still, Mason seemed happy enough.

As the afternoon wore on, the atmosphere in the streets grew seedier. Whores and drunks now pushed through the crowds and I suspected there was a fair amount of thieving as well. I was anxious to leave the city and get back to the ship. We reached the stable, hitched the cart to one of the horses, and, as quick as we could, made our way out of the town.

## CHAPTER FIFTEEN

### STEVEN BECKER
### THE WRECK OF THE Ten Sail

*I* might not have had the years, but I had been around long enough to know that when things are too easy, trouble is in the air. The second day of our return trip was uneventful and we camped by a small stream that night. I finally got as close to a full night's sleep as our watch schedule would allow and woke somewhat refreshed. But the dawn sky that morning showed red and we were without shelter. The only logical course was to make haste and hopefully reach the ship before the weather came ashore.

We were making good time, so good that I had almost forgotten the warning of the dawn sky. We returned the horses and soon we were pushing the cart the last mile to the beach. It was the kind of storm that came on you in a second. At sea, you could see them moving across the water, although there was rarely anything you could do about them except ride them out and try and avoid the waterspouts that accompanied the violent squalls. On land, though, there was less time to prepare.

The wind gave us a brief warning as it stirred the palm trees, but there was nothing to be done except put our heads down and push on. Within seconds the deluge filled the ruts dug into the path, instantly turning them to mud and cutting our speed by more than half. After only a few minutes, we were exhausted and stood to ease our backs and catch our breath.

The horsemen were upon us almost immediately. Without the bellowing of the storm, we could have heard them a good way off and cleared the road, but now it was too late. Even Blue was caught by surprise.

"You two, move on and no trouble will come to you," one of the men said, his floppy hat dripping water over his face. Without a word, another man trotted forward and lassoed Blue, tugging the line tight when it hit his waist. For such a small man, Blue was stronger and quicker than he looked, but was unable to escape the rope. The raider looped the end over the horn of the saddle and backed his horse away from us.

The visibility was so diminished by the rain that Blue and his captors were out of sight in seconds. I made a move to give chase, but Mason held me back.

"Nothing we can do," he said, holding me until they were long gone. As if its work were done, the rain ceased falling.

I stepped out of Mason's grip. "Well, we can't leave him." I threw up my hands in disgust at my inability to keep the crew together. Life was hard enough trying to shed the pirates' skin, but having a crew member taken hostage every time we seemed to accomplish something made the task impossible.

"We need to get this stuff back to the ship," Mason instructed. "Then we can mount a search party."

He was right. There was no other option. We dumped the water from the cart and put our backs to the work. Thankfully the ground had absorbed the rain and we were on the beach in under an hour. I waved to the *Panther*, hoping there was a watch.

"There was some activity on the beach here not too long ago, and it looks like the slaver's about to pull anchor," Rhames said as we pushed the skiff into the small surf. The water was flat and he had chosen to come alone to pick us up. "Thought I saw that little bugger of yours in the crowd of darkies they took on board."

I moved next to him on the bench so we could each pull an oar. The clouds were parting and the storm was moving west. Mason sat in the bow, his hand to his brow to cut the glare from the sun. "The slaver's raising anchor," he said.

From where we sat, I heard the chain scrape against the hull as the crew pulled it aboard, and then the snap of the sails catching the wind.

"Pull harder," I said as Rhames and I increased speed. Almost at the *Panther* now, I screamed at the top of my lungs to loose a volley and weigh anchor. The crew moved quickly, with Phillip and his daughter taking to the rigging to raise the sails and Swift and Red pulling the anchor. With the three of us still in the skiff, the ship was badly undermanned.

We were at the bow now. "Forget the anchor," I yelled. "Let them have a shot of the grape."

They ran for the cannon and I hoped they could get a shot at the slaver before she was out of range. It would take a lucky blast to cripple her, but it was worth a try, and grape shot was the best choice. A single ball had little chance of doing any damage, but the damage that could be inflicted by a well-placed smaller shot could disable a ship.

Rhames had done his part, and it was obvious the men had been busy in our absence. I saw stacks of shot and rocks from the stream wrapped in canvas bundles sized for a tight fit in the barrel. Several larger rocks were stacked nearby as well.

"Drop us here," I said to Rhames as I grabbed a rusty link.

"Mason, follow me." I started pulling myself hand over hand up the chain. The second I crested the rail, I yelled to the crew.

"Fire!"

The ship shook from the volley as I vaulted myself on deck. Quickly, I made my way to the capstan and helped haul the anchor aboard. Our mooring was shallow and the heavy hook came aboard quickly.

I patted Mason on the shoulder. "Take the wheel and have Rhames take charge of the munitions." He nodded and made his way to the helm as I jumped into the rigging. I had no pride in doing a seaman's work, and knew Rhames was better in battle and Mason was better with the ship.

I scurried up the rigging by the foremast and went to the spar of the topsail, almost falling when the ship rocked again from the guns. Smoke drifted up to conceal any view I had of the damage we may have caused. I raised the topsail, and before the wind could take it, I dropped to the main and raised it as well. The boat lurched forward, slowly picking up speed as the wind filled the sails. I dropped from the foremast rigging and went to the main, where I repeated the process. Mason had Swift and Red rigging the foresails, and within minutes we were under full canvas and in pursuit of the slaver.

I stayed in the rigging, straining to see if we had inflicted any damage on the other ship. If we had, she did not appear worse for it. Below, Rhames had the men organized into two crews, each packing powder, wadding and shot into the cannons, while Lucy and Shayla were busy replenishing the sacks of smaller rocks.

I dropped to the deck, gave each group encouragement, and went to the wheel, where Mason was fighting to keep the ship on course.

"That's a lot of sail in this breeze," he said as he fought the wheel. "Gaining on the bastards, though."

I glanced at the compass and saw our course was north. "He's heading to America," I said.

"Aye. That's where he can get the most coin for that cargo. Probably ride the stream up the coast of Florida and put into Savannah."

We should be able to catch him easily, I thought, but they must have known that, and would surely try to rid themselves of us. I watched their movement, trying to detect any change in course, then I retrieved the spyglass from the cabin and studied their ship. The deck was full of men, at least twice the size of our meager crew, but we were bow to stern and I couldn't see what they were doing.

I went into the main rigging and called to Mason, "Bring us off to the side." I locked my elbows in the rope ladder and tried to brace so my hands would be free to work the glass. The crew of the slaver were working in two teams, hauling cannon to the starboard side. Immediately I knew what they were up to and I dropped to the deck and called Rhames to the wheel.

"They mean to broadside us from their starboard side. They're moving the cannon across the deck now."

"Aye, they know we'll catch them. A crafty one that captain is," Rhames said.

"Right, then. He's thinking we're going to overtake him on the lee."

"If it were up to me, that's how I'd go at him. Better downwind and the ocean to my side instead of a reef," Mason said and turned the wheel to starboard. "I say let him think he's right and not give no indication to what we're up to. At the last minute, I'll cut behind and we'll broadside *him*."

Our cannons were on the port side. We would have to move and reset before we could take him. "He's going to be defenseless if we pull this off. I say we bring all four of our guns to starboard and take the chain to him with two. We won't get Blue back if we sink him. Be better to de-mast the bastard and then figure it out."

It was the "figure it out" part that bothered me as we got to work moving the guns. Shooting a length of chain from two different cannon could devastate a ship, but, even disabled, we would still have to board the slaver to get Blue back, and from what I had seen, they outmanned us two to one.

## CHAPTER SIXTEEN

STEVEN BECKER

THE WRECK OF THE
*Ten Sail*

The *Panther* closed fast, forcing Mason to change his course slightly to ease off the wind. We needed time for our plan to work. Normally, we would have reefed the sails, but that might alert the slaver to our ruse. With the change, the *Panther* matched the speed of the slaver, now less than a quarter of a mile away. The stench of her carried on the wind.

Our preparations were well underway; all four cannon were on the starboard side now. Rhames was in the process of securing and sighting them in. We would have to trust his expertise; there would be no chance to fire a test round. Our goal was to fire a broadside from one hundred yards, aimed into the rigging, so the guns were sighted above the waterline so as not to risk sinking the ship.

The two center carronades were placed ten feet apart, a length of chain draped over the rail between them attached to two projectiles in their barrels. The fore and aft guns might do some good, but it was the chain I was counting on to disable the ship. The charges were set and the flintlocks primed, but not cocked. The mechanisms for the center cannon were attached together with a lanyard, allowing one man to fire the chain. If packed correctly, they would shoot simultaneously.

The guns were ready, and I paced back and forth by the wheel, where Mason stood firm, steering the ship. There were still several hours of daylight left, but we needed to make our attack now. If it failed, we would need to muster another before night fell and we lost them. Mason slowly turned the wheel to port and waited for the sails to catch before correcting further. We picked up speed, and the gap began to close.

"Take the wheel," he said and ran to the hold.

He tossed the pump and hose onto the deck and barked orders to the men. One line was dropped into the water from the stern and the other lay on deck. Lucy and the girl were listening to his animated description of what they were to do, but I was too far away to hear and too worried about holding our course to care.

Mason was back at the wheel and all hands were ready at their stations as we closed to one hundred yards. We could hear the orders across the gap as the other boat likewise prepared for battle. I surveyed our situation and knew that if the cannon shot failed at its purpose, there was little we could do. With our skeleton crew and lack of proper arms, we were outgunned and undermanned. Having two women aboard only added to my concern.

There wasn't much for boarding gear on board, but we had found two grappling hooks that sat on the deck with a coil of line next to them, ready to swing when we came alongside. Fearing that boarding would result in disaster, I planned on holding them alongside with the threat of another broadside. We had agreed our goal was to take Blue back and leave the ship; none of us wanted any part of the slaver.

A single shot sounded and we ducked, expecting the projectile to slam into the deck, but it landed in the water on our port side. Mason held the wheel steady, relying on the headway we were making to quickly close the gap. It was a good tactic, as the next volley landed behind us.

It was time to make our move. We saw the men on the slaver ready at the guns on their starboard side and their captain with his arm raised, ready to give the command.

"Now!" I shouted.

Mason yanked the wheel and all hands focused ahead as we watched our bow swing to port. We were sailing close-hauled to the wind, a fast point of sail, and the two boats were within spitting distance and we came up on her at over eight knots.

I smiled as I watched the sudden panicked movements of the slaver's crew. Mason steered a few more degrees to port to give us the hundred-yard gap Rhames needed for accuracy. I drew a last breath, knowing the moment had come.

"Fire!" I yelled, and watched as Swift pulled the lanyard, releasing the flintlocks on the double gun, and turned away to protect his ears. Seconds later, the ship rocked and the cannon fired. I chanced a look but the smoke obscured my view. Something stung my arm and I ordered everyone down on the deck and to be ready with the grappling hooks.

When the smoke cleared, I crept to the rail to see if we had accomplished our goal. Shots fired again, but this time we were ready and returned fire. Another ball flew by my head, but I stood fast, chancing a look at our foe.

The foremast still stood, but the rigging was destroyed. Their mainmast was broken a third of the way up, exactly as Rhames had planned it. The slaver was dead in the water. Unfortunately, we were unable to maneuver without sending men into the rigging to drop some canvas, thereby exposing them to the slaver's muskets.

"The pump. Now!" Mason yelled. He handed the wheel over to me and ran to the pump, where he and Red furiously worked the levers.

As Phillip held the end, a trickle came, which quickly developed into a full stream of water.

"Hurry," I yelled now that I knew what the device was for. "Into the rigging and drop the topsails. Everyone else load the guns!"

I watched the flow of water increase and hit the deck of the other boat. It wasn't enough to do damage or harm a man, but it confounded their work and soaked their powder, rendering it worthless. I turned my attention to the helm. With the topsails down, we were more maneuverable, and I swung the bow toward the slaver to close the gap. Rhames called that the cannon were ready just as the hulls touched and the men threw the hooks. The water from the pump continued to spray, leaving them unable to fire.

"Ahoy," I yelled across the gap once we were secure. "Let's have the captain."

A smallish man appeared from behind the helm and called back to me.

"Our cannon are reloaded and ready to fire. Release our man and you are free to go."

While he talked to two of his men, Shayla came to my side. "You need to free them all."

I'd seen that look on a woman before and knew there was no negotiating. I called Rhames and Mason over.

Shayla needed no prompting. "The whole lot is dead meat if you don't save them," she said.

After Mason's past, I assumed he agreed with her. I looked at Rhames, waiting for an objection.

"We could use the crew," he said.

I was surprised, but he was right. I called again to the captain. "How many have you aboard?"

He looked up at me, "You could as well shoot me out of the water as take my cargo."

"Let's see my man now, and then I want an answer to my question," I replied. No one dared move or even breathe; the ships and their crews stood frozen. A man went below and came back a few minutes later with Blue. He released his shackles and pushed him towards the rail. I felt the girl move closer to me. "And the rest? How many?" I called louder.

"Two score below," he finally answered. "Me and another dozen make the crew."

Adding forty bodies to the ship would be close quarters, but we would be well manned. But what to do with them? I looked at Mason and Rhames, who nodded. Shayla merely stared at me in silence. "Send them up and you'll be on your way," I said. I worried that the tremor in my voice would betray me.

"But you'll ruin me," he cried back.

"At least you won't be on the bottom of the sea," Rhames shot back.

"You still have your ship," I added. "Fix your rigging and limp into port. I'm sure the likes of you will be back stealing men in no time." By now I had realized Shayla was right. Whatever the outcome, we had done the right thing.

He talked amongst his men for a few minutes, and I could tell by their hung heads that he would relinquish his cargo. An hour later, our deck crowded, we loosed the grapnels and drifted away from the slaver. The wind had just caught our sails when we heard the explosion.

## CHAPTER SEVENTEEN

*STEVEN BECKER*
*THE WRECK OF THE Ten Sail*

I could tell we were hit before the smoke cleared. The ship was listing badly to starboard, the same side the four tons of cannon were on. They had to be moved to port and fast. I ordered Rhames to organize the work, while I inspected the damage. I leaned over the side, oblivious to the small-arms fire now coming from the slaver. The splintered gash in the hull was clearly visible, wide as my wingspan, and reaching into the water.

"Swift and Red," I yelled, "take half the men below and start pumping for all you're worth."

Two dozen men, several barely able to walk, scurried across the deck and went into the hold. A few minutes later, a steady stream of water came from the scuppers, and a bucket gang formed to bail over the side. Our speed picked up slightly and the boat seemed to level. Rhames had two of the cannon over to the port side now. I evaluated the risk of leaving two guns on the starboard side and decided it was worth the weight. We could not leave the boat unprotected.

"Sight them in for fifty yards," I called to Rhames, who with Blue's help had the slaves on deck organized into an efficient labor force. It was hard to believe from their emaciated appearance that they were capable of such work, but newfound freedom does something for a man, and they had the scent of it.

I had to devise a patch for the hull, but first we had to deal with the threat from the slaver. Our ships were equals now, the additional speed we had gained from damaging their rigging now lost with the damage to the *Panther*'s hull. I looked over and saw men working on the slaver, running lines and repairing the spars. The mainmast was ruined, but with just the foresails, our ships kept pace with each other. I thought back to Gasparilla's lectures on naval warfare and racked my brain to remember a similar circumstance.

Night fell and still we beat into the wind toward the eastern end of Cuba, unable to escape the slaver. Lanterns lit their rigging and we could see the men still working at their repairs.

Under normal circumstances, we would have escaped into darkness, but, with the amount of water we were taking on, stealth was not an option. There was no way to quiet the pumps and the banging of buckets as the men fought the water. The men worked in shifts, about half at a time, Lucy and Shayla brought food and water to those who rested.

"We can't keep this up forever," I whispered to Rhames and Mason. "The men won't last the night."

"Aye, our situation gets worse by the hour, and theirs improves," Rhames said.

It was true. They were gaining on us now. Their three foresails were out, the main and topsail flew from the foremast, and they had just rigged the mainsail to the broken mast. We had few options and I grasped for the surest. The lanterns in the rigging gave me the idea. "We could set fire to them."

"And how are we going to do that? We'd have to be in sure cannon range to land a heated ball on her decks."

"Exactly," I said as the plan began to dawn on me. "Steer to port. We need to get upwind of her."

"That's going to put more water in her," Mason objected.

I knew it was the weather side, but we had the manpower and we would need the wind and seas for my plan to work. Both men nodded and followed my orders.

I laid out my plan, and a few minutes later a party of resting men brought the canoe on deck. I hated to sacrifice it, but there was no choice.

"Pack her with cotton and anything else that will burn," I explained. The old slaver was dark with tar and I expected she would easily catch fire. The trick was to reach her without notice.

The canoe was lowered over the port side as was the skiff, both out of sight of the slaver. Blue and I climbed down the ladder to the craft. We tied the canoe to the skiff with a small section of pitch-covered rope that went deep inside the cotton cargo. Rhames dropped a lit length of slow match down from the ship, and Blue covered it with a tarp to protect it from the water. Using the hull of the *Panther* to screen us from the slaver, I cast off the line and we started to row. It was hard work at first, working into the wind, but Mason veered off slightly and the ship lost momentum.

Slowly we drifted back. Mason was a master with a ship, and I trusted the change in course and speed had been subtle enough that the crew of the slaver hadn't seen us. Besides, distances were harder to judge in the dark. We soon heard the voices aboard the slaver. They hadn't noticed the course change and were clearly setting up for a broadside. Their captain thought his ship was fast enough to attack, but we had planned for that, and a few hundred yards before he could make his move, a shot fired from the *Panther*.

The carronade, fired from the stern, was purposefully aimed to port in an attempt to divert the slaver's attention while Blue and I slid into the gap between the ships. The crew moved to port as we'd planned, and we hooked onto the starboard side of their hull. An order was given and we heard the call of 'ready' from the crew. They intended to make their move.

## THE WRECK OF THE TEN SAIL

Blue and I were now hidden under the bow of the slaver. I gave my oar to him and picked up the grappling hook. My first shot missed and the hook hit the anchor chain. At the sound of metal against metal, I held my breath and waited a long moment to see if anyone had heard. It had gone unnoticed and I moved to try again. This time the grapnel floated through the gap between the hull and the chain, the hook hit the water, and I pulled back hard to create enough momentum for one of the points to snare a link. I leaned back, using the line to haul the canoe even with us, and tied it from the grapnel to a hole we had bored near its midpoint.

The ships were close now. We could hear the commands to ready the guns as the slaver prepared to broadside the *Panther*.

I tugged the pitch-laden painter towards me. The fuse started to burn as soon as I touched the slow match to it, and I waited until it reached the cotton. We had coated the cotton with pitch and oil, and it caught in a whoosh that ensconced Blue and me in flames. I felt intense heat on my face and smelled singed hair, but ignored it as I worked to wedge the canoe under the bow. It stuck, and fire licked at the wood and spread up the hull of the slaver. A smile on his face, Blue released the grapnel and we drifted away from the burning ship.

We waited, treading water with the oars, hoping the flames would be seen and preempt the order to fire. Then we saw it. The fire spread to the foresail and a crewman called the alarm. The mood on board changed after that and the attack was forgotten. The crew of the slaver was frantic, the men screaming at each other to save the ship. But it was too late. The first sail caught and the flames quickly jumped to the others. In seconds, the entire ship was ablaze.

Mason had dropped behind the slaver now and called out to us. I yelled back and soon we were aboard. Standing with the crew at the rail, we watched as the ship burned to the waterline and disappeared.

We were safe from the slaver, but not yet out of trouble. The maneuver had caused the hole in our side to widen, and the men fought hard to purge the incoming water. We needed a patch, but we were out of cotton and had no spare sails.

I ordered the crew to pry the deck boards from around the hold and asked Mason about the best way to make the repair. Without giving the order to adjust sail, he turned the wheel to port, and the bow moved through the center of the wind until the ship caught on the starboard tack. With the sheets still to port, she was hove to, barely making headway.

I took the wheel and watched Mason go over the side with Red and Swift in tow. A rope ladder led down to the skiff and was tied off at the bow and stern against the damaged section of the hull. There was nothing to be done except hold course while I listened to the hammering.

Once done, we changed course to the south—back to the Caymans.

## CHAPTER EIGHTEEN

Mason had the pump rigged as a wash station and was hosing the stench of the slaver off our new crewmen. We had to ration our food and water for the time being, but the freed men seemed satisfied. After they ate, Blue organized them to help work the ship.

The crew and I had discussed what to do with our new cargo. The men, from what we could tell, were stolen from Cuba and spoke mainly Spanish, with a little French mixed in. To a man, we decided they should be freed, but, in the interim, we could surely use the manpower to raise the treasure.

Twilight faded to night and I took the first watch. The ship was quiet now, the men scattered on the deck and throughout the hold. The adrenaline had finally left me and I relaxed at the wheel, enjoying the feel of the *Panther* as she cut through the small waves, throwing schools of flying fish off her bow wake. Shayla came on deck and put her arm around my waist, and for the moment I felt the thrill of victory.

I wanted to indulge in the moment and revel in the moment, but reality set in and I remembered Rory: was she a hostage, or the governor's ally? I started to move away from Shayla but her grasp was firm, and, at that moment, my mind and body were at odds with each other. My body won. We remained together at the helm for the rest of my watch, talking little, both needing time to process the day's events.

It was an easy sail on a beam reach, the wind steady and the seas calm. After a hard-won battle and with a woman by my side, I was lured into a sense of euphoria and I decided not to resist.

The next morning, I left Shayla, feeling a bit less bulletproof than I had the night before. I exchanged looks with the crew and sensed their approval as I walked the deck, inspecting their work. My tour took me to the hold, where brilliant white teeth smiled at me from the men sitting by the pumps. The patch had held and they now only had to work intermittently to keep the sea out. We would need to make a more permanent repair of the hull, but it could wait.

I went over to inspect our stores of powder and ammunition, wondering if I should post a guard. We were outnumbered badly, and though I had a good feeling about the freed slaves, I couldn't be sure if they were friend or foe. But after a quick look at the men on deck, I decided they had neither the energy nor the strength for an uprising. I would seek out Blue and see what he thought.

I met with Rhames and Mason at the helm to change the watch and decide what was to be done with the men. Our course would remain southerly, with a turn to the southwest before sunset. We would reef the sails overnight and make landfall the next morning.

"What of the men?" I asked.

We talked back and forth about the problem. It was decided that taking them back to Cuba was not an option. We might be branded slavers, a more dubious label than pirate, and the men might revolt, knowing they were returning to servitude. There were forty of them to our nine. They could overpower us by sheer numbers. A few might die in the attempt, but, as I had seen firsthand, men fighting for their freedom were willing to risk anything.

"What if we take them on?" I asked. After watching them work the pumps, I thought they might be a help. Besides, no one knew how hard it would be to recover the silver from the wreck.

"Have to bring in Red and Swift and see on their share," Rhames said before walking away.

Pirates had no aversion to slaves. Their crews often contained at least a handful of runaways.

"What about you?" I asked Mason, now that we were alone.

"I'm outvoted before we start as long as the pirates stay together, but I have no objection," he said. "Fact is, if any are good in the water, it might be a help."

Rhames was back with the other two men and we stood in an uncomfortable silence. The first order of business in settling shares and authority on a ship was to elect a captain. My heart stood in my throat as I waited for someone to speak.

"Reckon we ought to keep Nick as captain," Rhames said.

I breathed again. All present agreed and I took over the meeting. "Rhames ought to be quartermaster, and Mason, master of sail."

"Aye, but what of us?" Swift said, looking at Red.

"How about gunners at a share and a half?" I proposed.

"So we gets this straight. You get two and a half, and these two," he said, referring to Rhames and Mason, "they'll get two shares?"

"That's right. And the men that agree to swear an oath will get full shares," I said.

"Aye, but we're counting on you to make them big shares," Swift said.

"We've already lost a bloody fortune to the seas and the governor," Red added.

I was surprised they had elected me captain without first pressing this point. "I aim to get that back as well."

"We're agreed, then?" Rhames asked.

"There's one more. Phillip. I'd offer a share to start, but if he's useful, we can make it a share and a quarter," I said.

"If he's useful… meaning if we find the treasure in the wreck," Rhames stated. "Then we'll all be better off. I agree."

"How do you reckon to explain to the freed men how we run things?" Mason asked.

"I've got some Spanish, and Blue seems to be able to talk to them. Between us, I figure we can get the point across. If they see we're not going to put them in shackles and take them back to Cuba, I expect they'll agree to anything."

An hour later the full company gathered on deck. Mason, Rhames, and I stood on quarterdeck with Red, Swift, Phillip, Blue, and the women in front of us. I started in halting Spanish, fighting for each word until one of the men started laughing.

"Forgive me, sir," said the oldest of the lot, "but perhaps I could help." Something about the old man's bearing and the meat on his bones suggested he was more than a common slave.

"Your name, man?" I asked.

"They call me William, sir," he said in perfect English.

"And you can speak Spanish as well?"

"I can. I was in the service of a trader."

"Very well, then." I could only hope his translation was accurate.

"Please tell the men that they are free and we are willing to enlist their help in our enterprise."

He translated my words and a cheer came from the group. Before they got too excited, I decided to tell them the dangers they faced, and relayed this to William. His discourse was answered by smiles and nods. I assumed whatever unknown they were about to face was better than their previous lives. I explained our ship's chain of command, our plan to take the treasure, and how we intended to divide the spoils. The last bit was answered with a louder cheer. I stepped back to allow Rhames to assign the men their new duties and help them elect a leader for every ten men, someone who could receive and relay orders.

We finished and the assembly broke up. The men either went to their assigned duties or below to sleep.

"There's still one matter to be settled," Rhames said as I was about to go.

I was surprised it had taken him this long. "The girl."

"Aye, the girl."

"She'll be my responsibility," I said flatly.

I had my own suspicions about Rory and her betrayal, but that was none of Rhames's concern. For the time being, we had a more important problem to solve—how to raise the treasure.

# CHAPTER NINETEEN

### STEVEN BECKER

# THE WRECK OF THE *Ten Sail*

As we approached the island, Phillip was by the helm giving direction to Mason and pointing to the breaking white water. It was just past dawn and the reef looked ominous. It was so clearly marked, I wondered how ten ships could have been lulled into its embrace.

About a half mile from shore, a placid bay lay between the reef and the coast. It was still too dark to see the depth of the water in the sound, but Phillip had promised a narrow but deep pass to good anchorage. The shore looked inhospitable. It was easy to see from the bent trees that it was the weather side of the island. Their tops faced inland and their trunks were deformed from the relentless southeast wind.

"That's a dangerous bit to navigate," Mason said as he steered off the wind to gain sea room.

Phillip nodded and again assured us he knew these waters. We followed the southerly line of the reef, having to tack several times before we saw the island turn toward the west. Here the barrier extended even further out to sea.

"There." Phillip pointed to a gap in the breaking waves.

It was less than a hundred feet wide, but clearly gave access to the calmer water beyond. Mason tacked again to gain a better angle. Anything but a straight entry could wreck us on the adjacent reef. On a broad reach, we sailed through the gap in the coral and found ourselves in calm, clear water.

"Four fathoms." Swift called out the latest sounding from the bow.

Plenty of depth. I looked over at Mason. We nodded a silent agreement. This was as far as we dared venture without further exploration.

Mason called the order to drop anchor and, just as the iron hit the water, a school of spinner dolphins surfaced and swam next to us. I took this for a good sign, but remained cautious. I had Swift throw the wax lead all around the boat. He reported that it was shallow off our stern, but that the tallow in the bottom of the weight showed sandy bottom all around.

"Rig a cask and mark our position." I expected that we would be back and forth through here many times and didn't care to search for a new anchorage each time.

The ship settled back against the chain with the bow facing windward. I turned to shore and lined up several landmarks: a cluster of windblown trees to the south and a bluff to the right. I memorized the orientation of each to give quick reference if I suspected we were drifting. The men furled the sails and organized the sheets and rigging while Mason, Rhames, and I talked about how to proceed.

As we talked, I took up the spyglass to check the bluff to see if we had drifted. That's when I saw it. A silent puff of smoke, followed by the loud report of a canon and a ball slashing the water fifty yards to our stern. So much for the safety of the bay.

"Man the skiff," Rhames called.

I brought the glass back to my eye and studied the bluff. Several figures were running back and forth between two guns. It was too late to pull the anchor and escape. If we were within their range, we would know it in seconds. Another blast landed a bit closer and I ordered the men to add more chain to the anchor line. They did, and the ship crept towards the inlet, but remained anchored. The extra hundred feet gave us a bit of insurance. Again we waited.

Another shot fired and landed short. From what I could see through the glass, there were no more than four or five men manning the guns. Any more and they would have fired much faster. I signaled to Rhames, in the skiff. He tipped his hat and, with a dozen armed men, rowed hard toward the beach. The bluff might have been in range of our carronades, but we were left with only ballast stones and a bit of chain to shoot, not the gauged balls that would make the distance. Rhames and his men would land south of the gun placements and take the guns.

I ordered Red to take several men and rig a cable to pivot the ship on the anchor should we need to defend ourselves. Once the cable was rigged, I drilled two teams in how to use the device to take in or release line to move our guns to any angle an approaching ship could take.

As the men practiced with the cable, I heard a single pistol shot from the bluff. I grabbed the glass and went aft. This was our signal and I needed to see if the flag had been raised. Through the glass, I saw the small red pennant swinging in the breeze and relaxed, knowing that, at least for now, we had control of the guns. I would send two men back to the governor with a message that we were here, and that this was no act of piracy or war.

Once Rhames returned with the skiff, we commenced ferrying men to the beach to form hunting parties and take whatever water was at the battery on the bluff. With this many men, water was becoming an issue.

Only a skeleton crew remained onboard and Mason and I took the opportunity to lay out the gear we had purchased in Havana. The pump had already seen use and would have to be cleaned with fresh water. Blue and Lucy appeared surprisingly more interested in the equipment than hunting. They declined to go ashore and came over to help. Phillip worked with us as well, but there was no sign of Shayla.

I looked on as Mason laid the glass near the center of the oiled leather and cut a hole a few inches smaller than the square pane. We had searched the market for a round piece but had been forced to settle for square, but its quality was evident. With the glass placed over the canvas, he worked a piece of pliable metal to follow its contours, then rolled the excess material back over and used the hardware we had bought to clamp it in place.

"Fetch a keg of water," he called. "Seawater will do."

Phillip and I found an empty half-keg, attached a rope to it, and flung it into the bay. Once filled, we hauled it aboard and wrestled it over to Mason. He took the material and placed it over his head with the glass in front of his face, then plunged his head into the keg. A minute later he pulled back and removed the material, breathing in deeply.

"That was all I had for breath, but she didn't leak. That's the first test anyway. Now we need a core."

He grabbed a bucket from the deck, placed it over his head to see that it was the right fit, then smashed it on the deck. He took the bottom and two copper hoops from the debris and placed them inside the leather, then gave Lucy instructions to sew the lot together. "Just need a tie to keep the water out," he explained.

"A noose to keep the water out, you mean." I was amazed at what he appeared to be making.

He ignored the barb. "Let's see about rigging the air, then."

I followed him to the pump and watched while he adjusted the airflow before handing me the hose. "Now put this in your mouth and see how you can breathe."

I was reluctant, but there was little risk on deck. With the hose in my mouth, I gave him hand signals until I could easily breathe. It was easier than I expected once I got used to it. We had just finished calibrating the pump when Lucy came back with the helmet.

"When I get it on," Mason instructed, "stuff the hose under and place this loop around my neck. Pull her tight until I say." He took the helmet and placed it over his head, adjusting the glass piece until it was in front of his face.

He signaled and I pushed the hose underneath and tightened the loop. Phillip started to work the pump and I watched as Mason breathed. Several minutes later he gave me another signal and I removed the loop and helped him remove the gear.

"So it'll work just like that underwater?" I asked.

"Let's hope so. There'll be some things to be worked out, to be sure, but we can test it off the beach."

I felt ready to go right then, but the skiff was still gone. Our test would have to wait until morning.

## CHAPTER TWENTY

STEVEN BECKER

# THE WRECK OF THE *Ten Sail*

*I* rose before dawn, excited about our test. The skiff had returned after dark and our men's time ashore had not been wasted. Our stores were now full of turtle meat, and several casks of fresh water had been liberated from the battlement on the bluff.

Lucy had worked on the head cover through the night, and on inspection, it was much improved from the one we had quickly devised the day before. The seams were double-stitched and reinforced, helping to keep the metal bands in place. Two grommets allowed the hoses to be inserted directly. Mason said there would be leaks, but the pressure supplied by the pump would remove any water along with the spent air.

Mason, Lucy, Blue, and I piled the hoses, pump, and helmet aboard the skiff and rowed toward land. In the clear water, the bottom appeared much closer than it actually was, and it took three tries before we could anchor in head-deep water. Blue had volunteered to test the gear, allowing Mason and me to work the pump and observe from above.

Alas, the helmet was too big for him, so the plan changed

before we had begun and I placed the leather garb over my head. Mason briefed me on how he expected the apparatus to work, but until we were in the water it was all just words. With the tie in place, closing off the leather hood at my neck, I waited while he started to pump. After a few seconds the bellows pushed fresh air into the helmet and I began to breathe. Mason adjusted the pressure and, once I began to inhale easily, I gave him the prearranged thumbs-up sign.

Now it was time to get into the water. I climbed over the gunwale and landed feet first on the sandy bottom. The top of the headgear was just under the surface of the water and after a brief moment of panic, I raised a hand to signal that I was ready. Soon, fresh air surrounded me. I relaxed, took a deep breath, and submerged to my knees.

I was stunned by the clear view through the glass plate. Every contour of the bottom was as visible as if I was standing on terra firma. For a moment, I felt myself struggling to breathe, and I was about to shoot for the surface when I realized I was holding my breath. So I tentatively released the air in my lungs and inhaled the piped-in air. It tasted of leather, but I was breathing underwater.

Soon small fish darted past me. Entranced, I kneeled on the surface watching them. There were scores of them, but every movement was synchronized. I watched, mesmerized by the reflection of light off their silvery bodies as they swam. With my free hand I reached out to try and touch them, but, as one, they reversed course and shot away. A stingray appeared by my knees and I flinched when it turned its barbed tail toward me.

Mason must have thought something wrong when my other hand, the one we agreed should stay above water to signal, disappeared below the surface. I heard a muffled voice through the empty hose and yelled back that all was well. He must have misunderstood. I felt two pairs of hands grab hold of me and pull my head above the water.

"I'm fine," I yelled through the leather headgear and extended a thumbs-up. I wanted nothing more than to go back underwater, but Mason wouldn't let me. Despite my objections, he removed the gear.

"Let's go deeper," I said.

"Wait just a minute. This ain't no sightseeing expedition," he said. "We need to get the gear right. On your knees is one thing, but as soon as you start to go below a few fathoms, there are pressures to be accounted for. You need to take this for the serious business it is," he scolded.

I agreed, although I didn't understand what he meant by 'pressures.' I would have to trust his experience. Slowly we worked our way back to the ship, stopping several times to test the gear in deeper water along the way. The last test was at two fathoms, and I started to understand what he meant by pressure. At that depth, the quantity of air was inadequate and pushed the leather uncomfortably against my head.

"Air!" I yelled into the headgear, hoping that he would hear me above. By this time we had worked out our signal system to one-word commands. I distrusted using a tube for communication, but he must have understood because, seconds later, I could hear the hissing of the air entering the gear, and the leather expanded again. I breathed cautiously, more worried about my life than the surroundings now. If this is how things felt at twelve feet, I wondered how it would feel in the sixty feet of water the *Ludlow* rested in.

∼

Near noon, we sat in the skiff eating dried turtle meat and watching Blue yell in delight as he hand-lined fish using his share of the meat as bait. Before long, what space was left on the deck was covered in fish. We took the catch back to the ship, gathered a few more supplies, and went out for the last and deepest try of the day.

We were anchored just outside the small channel in thirty feet of water. The sea was different here, the bottom still visible, but where before, in the clear water inside the reef, you could see every grain of sand, only gradations of colors could be perceived here. Had it not been for the weighted line Mason had rigged, I would have panicked the minute the current grabbed hold of me.

The line was held firmly on the bottom by a heavy ballast stone. We had tied knots every five feet to mark the depth and I had just passed the third when I felt the water temperature drop. I swallowed hard and waited for the pressure in my ears to adjust before dropping two more knots.

With every fathom, the bottom became clearer. I was shocked at the color and magnificence of the coral structures. The majestic formations, so deadly to ships, were stunning underwater. And the fish! Thousands of them of all sizes and shapes swam all around me, darting in and out of the coral outcroppings. In my wildest dreams I had never imagined such a sight.

A call down the voice tube snapped me back to my reason for being here. I yelled back that I was all right, then continued making my way to the bottom. As I did, I relayed what information I could through the tube.

Mason wanted me to try and move away from the line to see how buoyant I would be at this depth, so when I was ready, I released my hold. Immediately I started ascending, my speed increased by the ballooning helmet, so I reached out, grabbed the line, and pulled myself back down to the bottom. The pressure was greater here. My ears ached, but the headgear returned to normal.

My heart was beating fast and I gulped for air. Finally I was able to slow my breath and I relaxed again. Off to the side, I saw what looked like a thousand fish moving as one toward the surface. Suddenly a flash of grey shot up from the depths, scattering the school. The beast swung his head side to side when he reached the outliers, scooping up the stunned fish in his open mouth.

The shark swam amidst the school, eating his fill. When he turned again, our eyes locked. A primal chill went up my spine as I stood helpless, watching this six-foot predator that had every advantage. With its head swinging side to side, it swam toward me. I thought to release the rope and shoot to the surface, but I was frozen in place. Then, just as suddenly as it had come, the shark turned and swam away.

∼

Back on the ship, we worked through the problems we had discovered during the dive. Diving on the wreck would require not only a smooth descent, but also a method to find and retrieve the remains. Not an easy task. For now, though, we put the latter problem aside and focused on the gear. Our most important task was to work on a weight system so the diver was not tethered to the rope line. After some adjustments, the gear was ready and Mason, Phillip, and I stood at the rail staring out to sea.

"She's over there," Phillip said, pointing past the reef.

Maybe he knew where the wreck lay, but from where I stood I could only see water. In forty feet, where he figured the deck of the ship to be, we would be hard-pressed to see the bottom unless the seas were dead calm.

"We're going to have to do better than that," Mason said, a worried look on his face. "We don't know if she's on the sand or the reef. The ship'll need to be right above her to service the diver."

"We'll just have to take our best shot," I said. "When we're near the spot, I'll go down and have a look." The image of the shark was still fresh in my mind. I wondered if there were even larger creatures further out, where the water was darker and deeper. I had already decided I would need to take some kind of weapon with me and talked to Blue about his thoughts on the matter.

"If it weren't for the reef, we could drag a chain between the ship and the skiff," Mason said.

Wreckers searching for a downed ship sometimes attached a length of chain between two craft and dragged it along the bottom until it caught on something. But with the reef visible above the waves, this system would be ineffective.

It was getting dark and I realized how tired I was. Because of my diving responsibilities, I had been taken off the watch schedule and had the entire night to rest. It was a rare luxury.

## CHAPTER TWENTY-ONE

STEVEN BECKER

# THE WRECK OF THE
# *Ten Sail*

Before dawn broke the next morning, I was already nervously pacing the deck, waiting for Mason to move the *Panther* and anchor her over the suspected site of the wreck.

My night had been restless, as my dreams were haunted by sharks and other demons of the sea, and my hours awake were full of thoughts of what could go wrong underwater. My only reprieve was a midnight visit from Shayla. Now, I was thankful for the daylight and the weather was turning out to be ideal for a dive.

It was hotter that day, but the lack of wind had settled the seas to a glassy calm, allowing us to see the bones of the wreck from the deck of the ship. What we didn't know was if it was the right wreck. When I felt the *Panther* swing on her anchor, I started to prepare the gear. We loaded it in the skiff, along with a spear Blue had whittled to ward off predators. The ship would offer support, but we had decided to use the skiff as a work platform. The small craft was cramped, but allowed for greater maneuverability and was closer to the water.

The headgear was salt-encrusted and stiff after the previous day's dive, making it even more uncomfortable when Mason and

Red placed it on my head and tied off the neck. It was hot and claustrophobic inside. Sweat poured off my brow, running into my eyes, making it hard to see through the already-cloudy glass. My breath came in gulps and I wondered if the heat would soon choke me. Finally, I felt the whoosh of air, gave the thumbs-up to Mason, and rolled awkwardly off the gunwale and into the water. We had tried several entry methods the day before, with mixed results. To prevent the headgear from slipping from my head, we had finally settled on a side roll.

It was a relief to be back in the water. The headgear lost its stiffness and the faceplate cleared. The cooler temperature settled me and my breathing evened out. I descended along the weighted line, counting the knots as they passed. I went slowly, allowing the pressure to settle in my ears before going lower. The lead had indicated we were in sixty feet of water, but the structure of the wreck was higher than the surrounding reef. Still, it would be deeper than I had gone the day before. If I had learned anything from that dive, it was that the deeper I went, the more things seemed to go wrong.

I forgot my worries the minute my feet hit the deck of the wreck. I'd imagined shipwrecks before and even seen some shallow ones from above, but until that moment, I never knew the life they attracted.

Thirty years of sea growth covered the ship, clinging to anything it could. Multicolored fish darted in and out of the open cavities while others pecked at the coral. I left the weighted line and started walking along the deck towards the hold. The weights Mason had hung from my belt held me to the bottom, and without any lines or sails, it was easier to move about the ship than I expected. Phillip had drawn a sketch of the ship, and I tried to orient myself before venturing inside. I still had no idea if this was indeed the *Ludlow*.

The hold was dark and I could see the antennae of a dozen lobsters hanging upside down from the deck. I stuck my hand out to grab one, but it moved backwards and out of reach. It was already darker in the deeper water, and I expected light was going to be even more of a problem inside the hold. With no light and unknown obstructions for the hoses to tangle on, I decided removing the deck boards and dropping in from above would be the best means of entry.

I moved amidships and went to my knees, ignoring the blunt-headed fish pecking at the coral next to me. The once-tight deck boards had decayed enough for me to slide my fingers between them, but when I went to pull one up, my fingers came back bloody from the coral crusted on them. I stayed where I was for a moment, watching my own blood float towards the surface. Hopefully no sharks were nearby to smell it.

I wiped my hands on my pants and rose to my feet. I was reluctant to go above, but it was probably time to report back. There was nothing more to be done. I would need tools and gloves to penetrate the wreck.

After two tugs on the line to signal the men to bring me up, they pulled and I rode the weighted line to the waiting skiff. On the surface, I suddenly felt heavy, but hands worked around me to remove the weights. Then I was pulled over the gunwale and the headgear was removed. Several voices asked me questions at the same time. I raised my hand to silence them until I could orient myself to the heat and light.

"Is it there?" Mason asked first.

"The decks are intact, but I'm going to have to pry the boards up with tools to access the bilge." I held up my bloody hands to illustrate that it was not an easy task.

"But it's there?" he asked again.

I shrugged, not knowing what to tell him. There were ten ships in the wreck and I had no idea if this was the right one. "We need to establish the provenance of the ship before we go any further," I said. "She looks like Phillip described, but there has to be something to identify her."

"She was newly launched," Phillip said. "It was her first voyage."

"Well, she's thirty years under the sea now. Every bit that hasn't rotted is covered with coral and barnacles."

He started to say something, but a blast from the cannon on shore drowned out his words. We had manned the battery and agreed that a shot would be fired from the bluff should a vessel approach. I stood in the skiff and strained to see what they had, but we were too close to the water.

"We need to get back to the ship," I said.

Mason and Red untied the weighted line that acted as the skiff's anchor and rowed us back to the *Panther*. Minutes later, we were on deck, and we saw the trouble. The sails of several ships were visible on the horizon.

Rhames came to my side. "We need to get inside the reef and within protection of the guns."

"Right, then," I said, grabbing the glass and climbing the rigging. "Make for the anchorage."

"Pull anchor!" Rhames shouted.

From high in the rigging, I could barely see the cask we had left floating on the line, but Mason would know the course. I looked down at the activity on the deck. Red and Swift were yelling orders to the new crew, and, with the additional manpower, we were underway in a matter of minutes. I had to twist in the rigging to see the approaching ships.

They flew the Union Jack, one a schooner, the other a frigate, but both larger than the *Panther*, and I had to assume better armed. Looking toward the cannon on the bluff, I estimated where we needed to anchor in order to be within their protection and out of range of the guns of the approaching ships. The shore-mounted guns could fire close to a mile, while even a well-winded carronade could only reach a quarter of that.

We entered the slot in the reef, and I briefly considered using our chain to create a boom across the narrow opening. Alas, there was no time. It was something I intended to do once we dispatched this threat.

"One hundred and fifty yards to my mark," I yelled down to Mason, pointing to where I wanted him to steer. From this height I could clearly see Swift calling the soundings and confirming the bottom was deep enough.

The two ships were already approaching the cut when we passed the keg. I waited another hundred yards before I called to the men to drop anchor. The lead ship was now making its way toward the cut and on her deck, I clearly saw the figure of the governor. A red-headed woman stood at his side.

## CHAPTER TWENTY-TWO

STEVEN BECKER

THE **WRECK** OF THE *Ten Sail*

Standing next to the governor, Rory looked stunning. Her dress was cut to her figure and accented by jewels that could only have come from our chests. I had never seen her like this and almost fell from my hold in the rigging when our ship swung on the anchor.

I felt someone climb next to me but ignored it and remained looking through the glass. I figured it was a crewman climbing to lash the topsail. That's when I smelled her next to me.

"I know you're not evaluating their readiness," I heard her say.

I froze as if I was doing something wrong, then, embarrassed, I moved the glass back and forth pretending to scan the deck.

"Let me see that."

Shayla pulled the glass from my hand and put it to her eye. I could tell she had never used one before by the way she jumped at seeing the figures up so close. I placed my arm on her shoulder to steady her and felt the warmth of her body.

"She wears the rouge of the whore," she said and handed the glass back to me.

Without waiting for a response, she climbed back to the deck, leaving me alone. I put the glass back to my eye and watched Rory again. She did appear different, her pale skin painted a reddish hue by the makeup.

I felt guilty for not evaluating the threat, and Shayla's reprimand had served to remind me of my duty.

The ship was a schooner, probably the governor's from the way she was appointed: slightly larger and better armed than the *Panther*. Uniformed crewmen scurried back and forth executing orders yelled from a man by the helm, clearly the captain. Behind the schooner, a larger frigate stood on patrol.

The captain called an order, and the men in the rigging dropped the schooner's sails just out of range of the cannons on the bluff. They were still in range of our carronades, but our bow was towards them. From this angle we would need to swing the ship to fire, but I wasn't yet ready to reveal the cable we had rigged.

As I made another pass over the deck, Rory again came into view. She looked back as if staring right at me, but her gaze dropped to the water and I saw her lips move. I followed her gaze to a skiff being lowered into the water. The captain and several armed men were aboard. I climbed back to the deck and ordered the men to stations.

While we waited for the boat to reach us, I played every scenario I could think of in my mind. Were they here to try and arrest us? The last conversation I had with the governor permitted us to salvage the wreck as long as the Crown got their share. Rory's presence, along with her dress and demeanor, had me wondering as well. She had acted demure and restrained during breakfast at the governor's house, but now she appeared to be the governor's woman.

"Put her from your mind," Mason said, now standing next to me at the rail.

I remained silent, watching the boat row closer. They were only a hundred yards away now.

"You want my advice?" Mason continued. "If it looks like a pig and snorts like a pig, it's a pig."

I knew he was right, but I still couldn't understand it.

Rhames approached and stood on my other side. I expected comment from him too, but he was all business.

"Do you want the men armed?" he asked.

I could see the cutlass hanging from his side and the pistol in his belt.

"Better wait. There's no threat yet."

Rhames seemed reluctant, but he held fast. For a pirate it was unnerving to watch the law approach and not flee.

"Ahoy," the captain called from the skiff.

They were next to us now, the two men at the oars holding water and keeping the boat in position by our ladder.

I called for one of the men to throw a line and allow them to tie up. "What can we do for you?" My voice almost cracked.

"Just a message from the governor: permission to come aboard?" the captain called back.

I debated the request for a moment but decided he posed no threat by himself. "Just you, then."

The captain wasted no time and climbed the ladder, his cutlass banging against the hull with each step. I held my hand out in the American fashion, but he just nodded and tipped his hat.

"You must be Nick," he said, ignoring my title.

"Aye. This is Mason and Rhames," I said, but Rhames had disappeared.

"Care to take a glass in my cabin?" I offered. I figured that what the captain had to say might be better heard in private.

"I'll gladly take the drink, but I'd prefer the air, if you don't mind."

I nodded to him and moved towards the companionway to get a bottle. Looking for Rhames, I saw Swift instead and motioned for him to follow me below.

"Check the cable and make sure the guns are ready," I told him.

I found a bottle of Madeira and brought it and three glasses back on deck. I wanted to steal a glance Swift's way to see if he was following my orders, but I thought better of it. Reaching Mason and the captain, I held the bottle out for inspection then commenced pouring.

I was unsure of the protocol for this kind of visit, so we drank in silence while I waited for the captain to take the lead.

He drained his glass in no time and pushed it forward for a refill.

"Looks like you've got yourself a crew," he finally said.

While he drank, I told him the story of the slaver.

After draining his second glass he came to the business at hand. "Well, I'm guessing you're wondering what this is about. Really a courtesy call is all."

I doubted that. I assumed the governor wanted control of his shore batteries back. The captain proved me right.

"You've got the rights to salvage the vessel so long as the Crown gets its cut, but you've no rights on shore."

I was ready for him. "We can allow an inspector aboard if you stand off," I said.

Before he could respond, I heard several splashes and a scrape against the hull from the men adjusting the cable. Hoping to distract the captain, I refilled his glass.

"Seems reasonable. You'll also not leave these waters without inspection, nor without the permission of the governor."

I had expected these terms and nodded. "And what of the girl?"

He laughed and drained his glass. "She's a feisty one, she is. Seems to have taken a liking to the governor." He winked.

"Right, then. The girl can make up her own mind, but I'd like to hear it from her mouth directly," I said, doing my best not to look at Mason. I knew his mind, but I still hoped things were not as they appeared.

I corked the wine. I was ready for the conversation to end. "If that is all, then," I said, extending an arm to the port rail. The captain took the cue and I let him go ahead of me. As he passed, I took a chance and looked towards the starboard side to see if the cable was secure. Swift gave me a nod.

At the port rail, I leaned over to watch the captain's descent. I was surprised how nimbly he navigated the ladder after the wine. Within minutes, the skiff was on its way back to the schooner.

With the captain gone, Rhames returned and he and Mason stood at the rail with me, watching the skiff. Suddenly we heard a boom from the battery and we ducked as the water exploded near us. Seconds later, the other gun fired with the same result.

"Get the men to stations!" I yelled and ran to the starboard side in time to see the schooner pivot on her anchor chain, showing us the guns on her starboard side. While I had been transfixed by Rory and entertaining the captain, the governor had laid a cable and taken the guns on the bluff. Now we were within easy range of both.

## CHAPTER TWENTY-THREE

STEVEN BECKER

### THE WRECK OF THE Ten Sail

They showed their broadside and fired two shots before I could even give the order for us to adjust our cable and show them our own guns. Fortunately, silence prevailed and I relaxed. It was only a show of strength.

I gathered the old crew together to admit my mistake in misjudging the governor. They all nodded and accepted our fate. At least I didn't have a mutiny on my hands. But we had precious little time to make a plan. A dory had already left the governor's schooner with four men in it. I wondered which of the men would be our guest—and the governor's spy.

The two men at oars I ruled out as seamen. The other two were contrasted in just about every way. The smaller man wasn't much bigger than Blue and had the look of an accountant. He looked seasick even in the light chop. The larger one was bigger than Mason, and looked like a bear, his ungroomed hair reaching down his back. He wore a heavy beard and went shirtless, showing the scars across his barrel chest.

"I've a bad feeling about this," I said as I continued to watch the boat. "The captain said a man, but it looks like we'll have two guests." Phillip took the glass and his whole demeanor changed. This had us worried.

"Phillip, what is it?"

He stammered, "Bad men, those two. They're like glue, each helping the other. The little one is the brains. He knows every secret on this island and beyond. And it's obvious what the big man does."

Without a word, Phillip grabbed Shayla by the arm and the two disappeared below deck.

Even Rhames looked troubled at what he was seeing. He could size up an opponent with a glance and this was not a good sign.

"Be hard to hide something with the two of them," Mason said. "One watching what we're bringing up and the other looking out for him."

"Right, then, I have no intention of hiding anything." I received queer looks from the three pirates. "Maybe we can use this to our advantage."

"How so?" Mason asked.

"With the governor and his men all on site, who's looking after our treasure?"

"Aye. Now you're thinking," Rhames said with a smirk. He ordered Red and Swift to help with the arriving guests.

I was now alone with Mason, Blue, and Lucy.

"Mason, can you go down and see what Phillip knows about our guests? I have an idea to get him off the ship and go with Blue to Bodden Town." The governor might suspect, but couldn't know for sure that Phillip was even aboard. "They won't be missed here," I continued. "The old man knows the layout and Blue can lead him and a small group of men to recover the treasure."

"What about Shayla?" Mason asked.

"Have her stay in my cabin and out of sight." I ignored the looks.

"And how are we going to get the treasure back?" Rhames asked.

"I'm going to invite myself to dinner with Rory and the governor. While I've got them distracted, put Phillip, Blue, and six men on the beach. They'll have to make a plan from there."

I went to the ladder to wait. Just as the accountant and his giant came on deck, I left them to Mason and climbed down to the dory. The crewmen looked at me strangely as I took a seat and cast off the line, but soon they were rowing back to the schooner as if it had been the plan all along.

That evening might be the last time I had any leverage with Bodden. With myself the only diver and the treasure still underwater, I had no doubt he would treat me well. I just hoped the governor and his captain would be distracted enough to allow Mason to put a crew ashore.

My confidence waned as we neared the schooner. The plan was foolhardy at best and I almost asked to turn back. My hands trembled as I climbed the ladder to the deck, but the captain bore a friendly face as he stood at the break in the rail, ready to help me aboard.

"Well, Master Nick," the captain said, his demeanor toward me obviously affected by the wine.

"I was hoping to have a word with the governor before we started the dive tomorrow. I have concerns for the girl," I said, playing the only card I had. The look in his eyes changed, but just for a second, and I wondered what he knew that I didn't.

"Wait here and I'll check if he'll see you," he said and walked away.

They kept me waiting, but I knew it was a ploy. It worked, though, and the wait was long enough for my confidence to vanish completely. I was scared. Not of what the governor would do—he was clearly a greedy man aiming only to enrich himself.

No, it was Rory. I tried to twist her actions any way they would bend to hide the obvious truth—she had betrayed me. On top of that, I felt guilty for sleeping with Shayla, and feared Rory would see it in my face. Countless scenarios played out in my mind, and none were good. Finally, the captain came back and escorted me below.

The governor's cabin was large and richly decorated. A table was set for four, and he and Rory were already seated. The captain moved to the seat facing the door, leaving me next to Rory. I took a chance and glanced at her, but she was laughing at a joke the governor told, oblivious to my presence. Whether it was purposeful or not, I didn't know, but it felt like a dagger through my heart.

"Good of you to join us, Nick," the governor said. "I might have extended the invitation myself, but as you are here, please enjoy." He toasted me with his glass before taking a drink.

I sat and fumbled with what I meant to say, but the rehearsed words wouldn't find their way to my lips. So I drank. The wine was sweet and potent, not at all like the liquor I was used to. I drank again, put down the glass, and cleared my throat.

"We had a deal," I started. "Now you have me penned in here, with spies aboard my ship."

"And what of it?" he said. "I'm just protecting my interests."

I knew that already, but I needed to find out for sure if Rory was one of those *interests*. "I understand, but I don't want our operation impeded by your men."

Bodden chuckled to himself as he refilled his glass. "That's not the reason you're here, Nick." He had a twinkle in his eye as he took a drink.

He had seen through me. I had to humor him without giving away too much. "I'm concerned for the well-being of the lady," I said.

Rory turned to me, her face bright red. "The lady is right here and can speak for herself—or is there another *lady?*"

How could she know? Oddly, her look of reproach made me hopeful that she did care after all. "Are you all right, then? I mean, well treated?"

Her anger seemed to suddenly vanish and she returned to the

THE WRECK OF THE TEN SAIL

icy behavior she had shown at breakfast the last time I had faced her. "Yes. Thank you. William has taken proper care of me. In fact, he has promised to take me to England with him when he retires there next year."

I searched her face, wondering if this was just another act, but when I looked at Bodden, he raised his glass and smiled again before taking Rory's hand. She did not resist and now acted as if I was no longer in the room.

There it was. She had chosen her path. The only interest she had in me now was as a means to enrich herself further. Dinner from then on was a miserable drawn-out affair. I suffered through, doing my best to make small talk and answer questions about the coming dive. After what seemed like an eternity, the captain finally rose and escorted me back to the dory. The governor didn't bother to rise and Rory turned her head the other way as I left.

As the men rowed me back, I thought about what I had expected from the encounter. Until then I had believed Rory was being held against her will. I'd half-expected her to make a furtive plea for me to save her or slip me a note with a secret plan of escape. But that was not the case. Instead it was clear she had formed an alliance with the governor. How far that extended I tried to put out of my mind.

I climbed aboard and looked for Mason. I found him at the helm.

"The men are ashore," he said. "We disguised Phillip and told our watchers we were sending a hunting party to check some traps we'd left for the boar in the interior of the island."

"How many?" I asked.

He lowered his voice. "Six was all we could manage: Phillip, Blue, and four handpicked men from the slaves. They're well armed. Phillip says it's a day's march to Bodden Town and they expect to be there by morning. They'll find the treasure and be back tomorrow night. We just need to keep the governor occupied until then."

I looked over at the two men standing by the rail. "And they suspected nothing?"

"Not a thing. Neither's a hunter, I'm guessing, because when Rhames said we needed to check the traps at night, they didn't call us on it." He smiled. "And besides, Rhames'll be watching them. He wants a piece of the big one. He's been sizing him up for a fight all night."

I said goodnight to Mason and went below, wondering if I should talk to Rhames. I decided against it. He would do no harm to the man until he had reason. There was too much treasure at stake. I entered my cabin and saw the candle burned almost to its base and, in the dim light, the curves of the girl in my bunk. Part of me wanted to leave her there, but when she rolled over, and the cover slipped from her body, it revealed more than I could ignore.

## CHAPTER TWENTY-FOUR

STEVEN BECKER
THE WRECK OF THE
Ten Sail

The next morning, under the watchful eyes of Bodden's spy, his henchman, and I assumed the governor himself, we moved off our mooring and left the sound. Half an hour later we anchored the *Panther* above the wreck site. We were out of range of the shore battery now, but the frigate had moved closer.

The dive equipment was loaded aboard the skiff and I was ready to board, but Mason stopped me.

"Best wait an hour or so until the sun is higher in the sky. You'll be able to see better," he said.

"I think you're just killing time," the small man said, poking his head around the helm.

I would have to be careful what I said while he was still aboard. I looked behind him at the dull eyes of the larger man and knew I couldn't ignore him—not yet. "Do you have a name?" I asked, frustrated I had to deal with him at all.

"Pott. James Pott. My friend here"—he twisted his mouth in an ugly sneer, revealing a row of black teeth—"is Gruber. And you've yet to answer my question."

"Well, Mr. Pott, as you were listening, you might have heard that Mason thinks it will be easier to see when the sun is higher."

"I heard him, but I have orders to see that this business gets finished quickly," he said. "No delays."

"Right, then. If you would like to put on the headgear and go have a look to see if there is enough light, we will assist you. If you'd rather I did it, then we'll wait an hour." I walked away.

I moved to the bow and watched the clouds forming over the land mass of the low island. It was going to rain later. That would be good for our fresh water supply, but it would hinder Phillip and Blue. I heard the unmistakable sound of an anchor being hauled in and looked seaward to where the schooner was preparing to depart.

Shayla joined me at the rail, carrying two cups of tea. We stood together in silence for a long minute. I couldn't help but notice the comfort I felt standing next to her, so different from Rory, who was always at odds with everything. I had reconciled myself with her actions the night before and held no animosity or hard feelings for her. I only felt confusion and hoped the path she had chosen was what she truly wanted, although I suspected she wanted less for me.

The schooner had her sails up and was through the cut. As we watched her turn south and disappear around the east end of the island, I hoped Phillip and Blue had accomplished their task and were on the way back.

"I've got to get ready," I said and handed the empty mug to her.

"Good luck, then," she said and squeezed me playfully. "Don't waste all your energy in the water."

I laughed to hide my concern. There was no need to tell her the schooner might make Bodden Town before her father could complete his mission. There was nothing I could do about that now, anyway.

I climbed down the ladder and waited for Mason to board the skiff. Looking up, I could see Pott standing by the rail watching me, and Gruber a few feet away from him. We had taken care to place the anchor right over the wreck, and the two crewmen pulled us to the anchor chain where it had been fastened. I stared down into the dark water.

The men helped me suit up and Mason explained that the two had experience in the water and would take turns free-diving to help me if I needed it. The communication tube could only be used for succinct commands, so he felt having a pair of eyes on me would help. I would be glad of the company.

The headgear was set in place, and Mason called to the men on the deck above to start pumping. I gave the thumbs-up signal when I felt the stream of air, and slid over the side. We had agreed to increase the weight tied to my waist, hoping it would make it easier to work on the deck down below. In addition to the weight, I had a long iron bar to use on the deck boards and as a weapon if need be.

The increased weight caused me to descend too fast and I could feel the pressure in my ears. I fought to clear them, swallowing hard every few seconds, but I was unable to bear it. I grabbed the weighted line and pulled myself back to the surface. With one hand clutching the gunwale, I removed the extra weight and shook my head back and forth. Mason understood and took the lead from me.

After a break on the surface to allow my heart to slow and my head to clear, I nodded that I was ready to descend again. Mason ordered the men to start the pump and fed the tether into the water behind me. This time I coasted to the bottom without incident.

Just as I hit the deck, I saw something shoot down from the surface. At first I thought it might be a shark and held the iron bar at the ready, but the shape turned out to be a man. It was one of the free-divers, and he was being pulled to the bottom by one of the extra weights. He reached me, handed over the lead, and kicked back to the surface.

My legs were heavy now with the extra weight, but I felt securely anchored to the deck, and I walked slowly toward the forward section of the hold. With the iron bar I started to pry the deck apart and watched as the boards floated loose, carrying with them a cloud of brown dust.

I waited for the water to clear up, jumping back and dropping the bar when a long silver fish with two huge fangs for teeth shot towards me from the gap. Its eyes met mine for an instant before it turned away and disappeared. I waited a minute to see if there were any other predators hidden in the hold, but none followed. I retrieved the bar, pried another few boards loose, and stood back just in case another fish lurked below. A half dozen boards later, I was able to kneel down and look into the hold.

There was little light, and I knew I would have to remove more boards, but I could see the ballast piled in the bilge not ten feet below me. Whether or not it was the silver ballast of legend I didn't know, but being only feet above it made my heart race. The rest of the deck boards came off easily and soon the entire bilge was open.

The two crewmen had been taking turns checking on me, using the weighted line to descend in order to save energy, but I needed the line now. With the extra weight I wore, I wouldn't have a way to escape from the hold without it. I signaled the man over, and we looked each other in the eye, a very strange feeling underwater. I pointed to the line and then to the hold, and he seemed to understand. He held up a single finger, indicating to me that he would send the other man to do the work.

A few minutes later the weighted line was in the bilge. I grabbed hold of it and descended the remaining ten feet, landing on the ballast.

My heart sank.

It all appeared to be stone encrusted with growth from the reef. No silver shone back at me. Either it was the wrong ship or we had come here for nothing. Defeated, I pulled myself up the line to the skiff.

Mason and the crewmen pulled me aboard and removed the headgear. I sat on deck catching my breath while both men waited patiently, anxious to know what I had found.

"Stone," I said, trying to slow my breath. "It's all just stone."

"Stone?" Mason echoed. The disappointment was clear on his face.

"Looks that way. All covered with barnacles and sea life."

Mason thought for a moment and then looked at me. "Any of it look dark, maybe black?"

I thought back to what I had seen and, although I couldn't answer for sure, I remembered that the lower stones appeared black in the light. I looked at Mason and nodded.

"I should have told you what the seawater does to silver. Just a few days of it'll start to hide the shine and turn the metal black. Over time, it forms a casing."

That could have been what I had seen. Suddenly I felt invigorated. I moved to grab the headgear when Mason put his hand on my arm.

"Maybe we ought to play this as a loss for a bit. Might be better if we know what we have before they do. The minute you bring something up, they'll be on us."

I agreed. We needed to delay, at least until Phillip and Blue returned. But the treasure was too close. I had to know. "What if I take a knife and scrape the stones down there?"

"That'll work." He smiled.

"Keep a watch for Phillip and Blue," I said before I put on the helmet and tumbled back into the sea. With the pry bar in one hand and a knife in the other, I followed the weighted line into the hold and stood again on the stones. The light was better now with the sun directly overhead, and I used the bar to move the ballast apart. Some coral broke free, creating a cloud of silt. I had to wait for it to settle before I could see what was there.

It seemed to take forever for the stones to come back into view. I busied myself with watching the sea life, but I was unable to enjoy it as I anxiously glanced back at the pile every few seconds. Finally the silt settled and I got on my knees to examine the stones. The first two I took the knife to revealed only granite, but the third was different. The black casing fell away, revealing the dull glint of silver.

## CHAPTER TWENTY-FIVE

STEVEN BECKER

# THE WRECK OF THE *Ten Sail*

I skipped the last rung on the ladder and set foot on the deck of the *Panther*, doing my best to look disappointed. Mason knew what I had found, but we had decided there was nothing to be gained from revealing what we had found until Phillip and Blue returned. Pott stood in front of me with Gruber just behind him, barely giving me enough room to step on deck.

"Well?" Pott asked.

The Grub, as the crew had taken to calling him, leaned over the little man's shoulder and I swore I could smell his foul breath from three feet away. I shook my head and lowered it to conceal my face. "Just stone."

"It has to be there," he insisted. "You must dive again."

Gruber nodded behind him.

"He'll go when he's rested and ready," Rhames said, coming toward us and forcing his body between the two men and me.

He and Gruber exchanged looks and I knew before this affair was over, it would end badly for one of them. The sky darkened and we all looked at once to the thunderhead blocking the sun. It was moving toward us with the top of the anvil reaching high into the sky. A grey wall of rain could be seen streaming from its tail.

"We'll have to wait out the storm," I said.

"It ain't storming under water," Pott said.

I took another look at the storm to buy some time and thought I saw a small sail, just a dot on the horizon, trailing behind it. "Let me eat something and I'll go have another look."

I pushed past the little man, causing him to back into Gruber, who in turn pushed Rhames. The two men squared off, each ready to fight. "Not now," I called to Rhames, who gritted his teeth, but obeyed. "You and Mason come down with me."

Pott objected. "There'll be none of these private meetings on my watch. The governor's put me here to see that everything is aboveboard. If you have something to say to these men, it should be said in front of me," Pott spat.

Gruber, empowered by my restraint of Rhames, nodded his approval.

Rhames looked at me again with a pleading look on his face, but I shook my head.

"Right, then," I said, turning so their backs were to the storm and the approaching ship. It was a single sail clearly outlined by the grey backdrop. I strained to see if it flew the red pennant that was our signal, but it was too far away. "I'm going down to get some food. Why don't you gentlemen join me and we can review the afternoon's dive." I placed Swift at the helm, with a quiet word to alert me on the progress of the ship, and led the procession below.

Shayla was in the galley, but on seeing Pott and Gruber enter, she disappeared. Pott noticed. I could see the calculating look on his face, but he said nothing. We sat and ate the fish she had been preparing. I needed to buy some time and I was ravenous from the dive, so it wasn't hard to delay conversation until the food was gone.

"You have a plan, then?" Pott asked, his impatience showing.

There was something odd about the man. Whenever he spoke, his face contorted as if he were in a great deal of pain. I had seated myself to allow a clear view of the companionway, hoping to catch a sign from Swift, but the opening showed only grey sky.

"I might have another look," I finally said.

"How many looks do you need before we move and look somewhere else? It seems to me you're stalling."

I glanced again at the companionway, but this time he saw me.

"What's that you're looking for?" he asked, rising to his feet.

The big man got up behind him, pushing the table into Rhames and Mason. I gave Rhames another look to restrain him, but knew his fuse was getting short. We had no choice but to follow the two men on deck.

I chanced a look at where I thought the ship should have been, but the storm had moved between us, and the seas had increased from the wind accompanying the weather.

"He's right," I said. "One more try and we'll move on." There were several other squalls on the horizon, but it was pointless to wait them out. They would do what they would.

I climbed down the ladder to the skiff and waited for Mason and the two crewmen to help me suit up. Pott and Gruber leaned over the rail again, watching. At least their attention would be diverted from the ship, which, if it was our men, would be approaching from the starboard side. Two crewmen joined Mason and me in the skiff and I was soon underwater again.

We'd had a quiet word about what to do with the silver and had decided to pile it on the wreck's deck. We would have to determine the best time to bring it up.

I landed on the deck of the sunken ship. The weighted line was beside me and I took it to the bilge, where I placed my hand loosely around it and dropped into darkness. On my knees, I felt around for the silver ballast stone. Finding it, I pulled it from the pile and set it to the side. The hold grew darker and I looked up apprehensively. It was just a cloud shielding the sun, but it was hard to see now. Fortunately, the shape of the silver casting was easy to identify, and I began removing the pieces that felt right.

One by one I brought them up and piled them on the deck of the *Ludlow*. I was sweating from the exertion, and the faceplate had fogged up, making it hard to see. My breath came in huge gulps as I tried to replenish my lungs. Exhausted, I placed the last of the silver blocks on the deck and pulled on the line, our signal that I was finished. Nothing happened and I realized that neither of the divers had been down in a while. I pulled again and waited, wondering what was wrong.

Without warning, the makeshift helmet collapsed around my head, and I was suddenly unable to breathe. Something was going on above, but I couldn't afford to wait.

Holding my breath, I started to pull myself up the line but I made little progress. I began to panic, until I remembered the weights around my waist. I released the belt, and without the burden, I moved quickly up the rope, straining my head in the gear to scan the surface for activity. The water was churning around the skiff but, unable to release the headgear without help, I continued up the rope until my head broke the surface.

"Hurry up, Nick!" Mason said as the men grabbed me under the arms and pulled me aboard the skiff. "The pinnace is in the bay."

I tried to turn, but the headgear restricted my movement until the two crewmen released the tie and removed it. After at least an hour underwater, even the cloudy sky blinded me. I squinted towards the cut and saw the small boat bobbing on her anchor.

My eyes adjusted and I turned to Mason. "Was she flying the red flag?"

"She was." Mason nodded, dropping the line in the water and releasing the anchor line.

While the crewmen rowed back, I tried to put the pieces together. The pinnace had flown the red pennant, meaning Phillip and Blue controlled her, and they must have the treasure or they would never have risked stealing the boat. Without the weight of the chests, they could have easily made it back undetected by land.

I looked back at the single-masted ship and saw it was inside the reef, well within range of the shore battery. Not sure who controlled the guns, I could not dismiss the threat, though I doubted that the governor would risk firing on them with the treasure aboard.

"Why are they inside the reef?" I asked Mason as we pulled our way back to the ladder.

"Storm drove them in," he said, following me up the side of the ship.

We had just reached the deck when Pott ran to me. "That's the governor's pinnace," he shouted. "The red flag is no signal of ours! What trickery are you men up to?" He turned to me, his stinking breath scorching my face.

Before I could speak, a loud boom sounded and lightning struck just outside the reef. There was nothing we could do but find cover and ride out the storm.

## CHAPTER TWENTY-SIX

STEVEN BECKER

# THE WRECK OF THE Ten Sail

The squall had finally spent itself, and one by one we rose from where we had found protection from the storm. A light rain continued, but sunlight started to filter through the clouds as they moved out to sea. My first thought was of the pinnace, but as I looked toward the sound, another ship caught my eye. The frigate was back, moving into position to block the entrance to the cut. Our men had been spotted and were now bottled up inside the reef.

The *Panther* was still anchored over the wreck on the far side of the reef, in no position to help. We could pull anchor and escape, but with our treasure bottled up in the harbor and the silver still at the bottom, that plan was not to our liking. We had to fight.

"Weigh anchor," I ordered. There was no way we would sit and remain an easy target. Once we were mobile, our options would increase.

"No!" shouted Pott before he looked at his protector, issued an unspoken order, and ran for the companionway.

Gruber moved to the bow and forced his way through the men who were busy hauling the anchor chain around the capstan.

## THE WRECK OF THE TEN SAIL

Swinging both arms, he lashed at the men, forcing them away from their work.

"Open the arms chest," I yelled. "He can't fight us all at once."

I ran to the stern, where Rhames met me and used the key around his neck to unlock our weapons. We each grabbed a sword and made for the bow. As we passed the companionway, I saw Pott emerge with a pistol in each hand.

He pointed one gun directly at me. "Maybe we should have a talk before you go and do something stupid and get us all killed," he said and motioned me to the helm.

We stood together by the wheel, the pistol still aimed at my head. Without looking, he turned his left hand to starboard and fired a shot towards the governor's ship. I wondered what he was up to.

At its apex, his shot exploded into a brilliant flash of orange. It was clearly a signal to the other vessels.

"Make the skiff ready," he said, the barrel of the other gun still trained on me. "Gruber, let's go," he called to the bow before walking backwards toward the ladder. "Get those men up here," he said to me.

The two crewmen were still aboard the skiff waiting for orders. Instead of ordering them to tie up, I did the opposite. "Stand off one hundred yards," I ordered. The men looked confused but did as I asked. We stood in silence watching the skiff move away.

"That wasn't what I asked," Pott barked, jabbing the gun into my temple.

"You only have one shot," I said, feeling braver than I felt. "Go ahead. Your man can't hold off this many men."

I could tell from the look in his eye that I had won, but now the frigate was underway and moving toward us.

"Right, then. Let's get on with it." I went for the wheel, and Rhames went to the bow with several armed men in his wake.

"I'll handle the Grub," he called to me.

I knew he had been waiting for this moment, and I let him have his way. "Raise sail," I yelled to the men in the rigging, who were watching the action below. It was good to have a full crew. I wasn't sure how skilled they would be as seamen if we needed to maneuver in tight quarters, but at least we had the numbers.

The mainsail filled and the anchor chain groaned under the strain, but it still held. There was nothing I could do from the helm but watch until Rhames removed the giant and raised the anchor. The men parted as he made his way forward and he stood face to face with Gruber. A smile crossed his face for a brief second and he raised his sword.

"Stand back," he ordered the men. "I'll handle this." Then Rhames charged the giant.

Gruber blocked his charge with a downward chop, then sidestepped, out of the way faster than I thought was possible for a man of his size. Rhames turned back, his smile gone.

I yelled a warning when Gruber reached behind him and grabbed the fire axe mounted on the mast. He slashed back and forth, moving closer to Rhames with each swing. The men moved out of the way, snarling insults and circling each other. It was just the two of them in a standoff by the forepeak. I realized that the way to the anchor was clear, and I called to the other men.

"Never mind them," I ordered. "Raise the anchor."

After a moment, I felt the anchor break free and I suddenly had control of the wheel. I saw the two men trading blows, with Gruber slashing furiously at Rhames, who was down on one knee and unable to counter. I gave the order to come about and looked ahead to start our turn through the wind.

My only hope was that the larger man knew little about sailing and Rhames could take advantage of the unexpected movement of the ship. "Coming about," I yelled as the men in the rigging ducked under the stays and the sails snapped around.

Rhames knew what was coming and used the momentum of the turn to roll to the side of the man, who was thrown off balance from the ship's sudden change of course. Just as Rhames came back to his feet, he cut a low blow to Gruber's ankles. Blood spurted from his Achilles tendons and the man screamed as he fell to the deck. With a diving lunge, Rhames finished him.

At the same moment, a shot fired by my head, and my ear exploded in pain. I had forgotten about Pott. I checked my head to make sure it hadn't been blown open, but there was no blood and I still had my wits about me. I turned to where he had stood and saw Shayla standing above the rodent, holding a saber to his throat.

"I have the wheel," Mason yelled. I barely heard him through the ringing in my ears and moved out of the way.

There was no time to thank Shayla, but the quick look we exchanged said enough. She was about to stab him again, but I caught her arm with my hand, stopping the blow.

"Bastard deserves to die," she hissed.

"That he does, but we need him to bear witness first. He's a king's man and we'll need his testimony to clear our names."

I felt her relax and she let me take the blade from her. Pott was rolling on the deck, hugging his wounded arm to his chest. I looked for Lucy to doctor him, but remembered she was on the pinnace.

"I'll handle it," Shayla said, "but it won't be pleasant."

# CHAPTER TWENTY-SEVEN

STEVEN BECKER

THE WRECK OF THE
*Ten Sail*

We could little afford to try and match broadsides with the schooner. They had at least twice the guns and a more experienced crew. Evasion and trickery had worked for us before, and it would have to again.

The girl had enlisted several crewmen to get Pott below, and the body of Gruber was tossed overboard, food for whatever sharks wanted a piece of that foul meat. With the governor's men gone, we could speak freely.

"Turn to starboard," I called to Mason and went into the rigging for a better vantage point. We had been on an easterly course, away from land. This would make sense to the crew of the schooner, as their captain would assume we were trying to lure them away from the pinnace trapped inside the reef. But Phillip had drawn a sketch of the water surrounding us, including another exit from the sound. He wasn't sure of the depth, but after my time underwater, I had an idea how to enlarge it.

"What have you in mind?" Mason called back.

"Through the cut and into the bay. The frigate draws too much water to follow," I called back.

"I hope you know what you're doing," he said, loud enough for too many men to hear.

I ignored his doubts. "Get two men on the lead and hug the reef."

I judged the range of the cannons on shore, and I had to assume the governor had sent men to secure them after discovering the theft. I turned to see how the frigate had reacted to our course change. As I hoped, they were preparing to shoot to starboard, not toward land, but their preparations had been to the wrong side. With the wind behind them, the only move the captain would have would be to jibe, and that wouldn't correct the situation for him. His ship was larger than ours, and I was counting on its deeper draft to keep him out of the sound and away from the reef.

The water gradually lightened in color, and from my perch the sand became visible. The schooner had executed her jibe and corrected course. They were close enough to fire and I could see the men on deck now frantically preparing the port guns, but we had minutes before they would be ready. We were into the cut now and Mason made a slow turn northward. The sheets were adjusted for a broad reach and the ship picked up speed.

There was no way to signal my intentions. I had only to rely on the men in the pinnace to see our move and react accordingly. Their anchor was already up and they had the main and a jib set. Together we made our way north toward the sound and I could only hope Phillip knew where the exit was. I looked out to sea and saw the frigate standing off the cut, waiting for us to turn and try to make a run for it.

Back on deck, I went to the helm and asked Mason to drop speed and let the smaller boat catch us. The pinnace had a much shallower draft and we needed Phillip to navigate. As they pulled alongside, I went to the rail to explain my plan.

We had to shorten sail to stay behind the slower boat, but it didn't matter. I looked back and the frigate was still standing off the cut, thinking it our only chance to escape. The sound was small enough that they could see every move we made, but I hoped to put enough space between us for us to evade them when we finally made our exit.

The water grew shallower, the reef closer, and I saw no sign of a passage through the crashing waves. The pinnace dropped back and I ordered the men to lower the mainsails. The call from the bow was three fathoms. I could not allow the boat to get closer to the reef without some indication it was safe.

"It's here," Phillip yelled from the pinnace.

"Head through and signal back the depth," I yelled back.

"Then what?" Phillip replied.

"Then turn to the north. If we don't catch you, you'll know our fate."

As ordered, they pulled ahead of us and were soon through the reef, into deeper water and about to make the turn. The frigate was sure to have noticed the pinnace escape and would have to commit to either following them and the treasure or staying with us. It was time for my plan.

"Turn ten degrees to port and set the elevation on the guns as low as it'll go." I waited until they called back that they were ready. "Prepare to fire," I yelled. I got some strange looks from the crewmen, but they followed the order.

"Think it'll work?" Mason asked, and I saw the worried look on his face.

"If this bit of reef is like what I've seen, anything standing off the sea bottom will succumb to the shot."

I heard Rhames call ready. The ship remained frozen in time as I waited for a wave to pass beneath the hull and give the guns the downward angle they needed. The bow was just about to hit the white water, and the men were staring at me. Finally the hull moved up on the crest of a wave, and I had the angle I needed.

"Fire!" Several seconds passed and the wave continued through us. We were past the crest and on the back side of the wave when the guns erupted, shooting water high into the air. There was no telling what damage we had done to the coral until we approached.

We were in the reef playing the gambit under full sail. I climbed back into the rigging for a better view and assigned two men to work the lead. It would only take one of the coral pillars to tear the bottom from the boat.

The ship moved slowly through the reef but the water was clouded with silt from the shot and I was unable to see the bottom. I climbed down, imagining the damage we had caused and hoping it would be enough. There was no way to know. I was so tense that, when a larger wave rocked the ship, I almost lost my balance.

Before I knew it, a cheer went up from the deck, and I knew from the direction of the swell that we had made it through. The land was on my left over the port rail and Mason turned north to follow the pinnace.

I looked back at the frigate, but they were now too far behind to catch us. "Ease off the sails," I ordered.

"What do you mean?" Rhames and Mason both looked at me like I was crazy.

"If it's the pinnace he wants, let him see the tip of our masts," I said. "We'll move around the point, wait for night and, at dark, anchor in the mouth of the bay."

Their blank stares told me I needed to explain more.

"Look, we can't be stealing his boat. I have a plan to take our treasure, retrieve the silver, and get away clean. Then we'll make the first British port and march Pott in to make a statement. It'll cost a bit of silver, as was our agreement with the governor, but there's a ton down there. We'll have to toss some of our ballast just to carry it."

"You trust that worm?" Rhames asked.

"I trust him to save his own skin." I was sure that without his protector the man would do whatever I asked.

The sun had just slipped below the horizon when we anchored in the mouth of the bay. I climbed the rigging with the spyglass and saw the frigate rounding the point and heading our way. We had an hour at best to execute my plan.

Lanterns were lit on the pinnace but my orders were that there would be no light on the *Panther*. I wanted the captain of the frigate to think we had run. But just in case he sensed our ploy, I set two crews on the guns and placed watches in the rigging. We drifted in the mouth of the bay with the pinnace tied to our side waiting for Swift, Red, Rhames, and Phillip to offload our treasure.

While they worked, I went below and wrote a note to the governor. I explained in clear language that we held Pott and that his protector was dead. At our next port of call, Pott would attest to our innocence. I signed the letter, ran above deck, and jumped the rail. Then, with the butt of my dagger, I nailed the letter to the wheel of the pinnace.

"Hurry, men," I called, now that darkness had enveloped us. The schooner was a half mile away and it was time to make our move. I called to Mason to untie the ships and we slipped away, leaving the pinnace to drift and making it that much harder to recover. So long as we escaped unobserved, I had no doubt that the captain of the frigate would be unable to resist the lure of the pinnace.

"All quiet now," I called and the ship became silent as we glided out to sea. We had the wind at our back and we were quickly picking up speed. From the angle she was heading, I figured the frigate would have to tack at least twice to reach the pinnace, giving us ample time to disappear below the horizon.

I stared off the stern until the lanterns from the schooner merged with the lights of the pinnace, then I watched them slip below the horizon. Feeling relieved for the moment, I steeled myself for the night ahead. I meant to do what had ruined many ships before.

## CHAPTER TWENTY-EIGHT

STEVEN BECKER

THE WRECK OF THE
*Ten Sail*

My eyesight was better than most of the crew and I rested against the spar of the topsail, scanning the dark water. We had tacked out to the northeast, away from the island, in order to avoid the frigate. Once I was sure we were out of sight, we changed our course to the southwest in order to head back to the wreck. It was not lost on me that the ten ships whose bones lay under this same reef had run aground at night.

I had been staring into the blackness for what felt like hours, searching for the coast. The moon would be up in an hour, but for now, I just stared blankly toward where I expected the reef to be, hoping for a glimpse of white water before it took us. We were still running dark and I knew every man on deck was listening for the sound of waves crashing on rocks.

My trance was broken by Shayla. The rigging swayed unnaturally, and I looked down to see her climbing up the rope ladder to where I stood on the spar of the mainsail. She was nimble, and although I was neglecting my duty, I couldn't help but watch her.

"Care for some company?" she asked as she reached me.

"I could use another set of eyes, for sure," I said.

"Not what I was wanting to hear, but I'll stay just the same," she said.

"It's not what I meant," I said, fumbling my words.

Shayla climbed beside me and I felt her hand around my back.

"You've no regrets about leaving that red-headed trollop behind?" she asked.

I knew sooner or later we would have this conversation. I almost jumped to Rory's defense, but when I remembered our last meeting, I caught myself. I had seen nothing from her to tell me otherwise, and I had held out hope for her long enough.

"No regrets," I said and turned from her to search again for the shore.

It was a lie, of course. I did have regrets and I was still confused. Rory and I had been together for several months, and although nothing had happened between us, I had thought of her as my woman. But now, in the darkness, I realized I'd been wrong all along. She had always been looking for the first opportunity to leave us.

Shayla hugged me tighter and I reveled in the closeness.

"Look, the moon is rising," she said, pointing to sea.

I glanced back and we watched the near-full moon rise above the water, leaving a phosphorescent trail in our wake. I thrilled to the beauty of the moment.

"Do you hear that?" she asked.

I turned my attention back to my search for land. I listened and was about to ask what, when I heard it too: the sound of waves. Phillip had warned me of two points to watch for where the reef came right to the shore before reaching out to sea. Sailing too close to either of those points would ground us.

"Ten degrees to port!" I called down, breaking the silence on deck. The boat came to life with the sighting.

"Aye, I see it now," Mason called back to me.

"Have Phillip guide you. I'll be right down," I shouted.

I moved to descend the rigging, but as I stepped in front of

Shayla, She grabbed me with both hands around the waist, leaned in, and kissed me.

∽

*O*nce I was sure we had cleared the point, I allowed a small lantern by the binnacle to see the compass, but otherwise, we remained dark and quiet. Conscious of the reef to our right, Mason gave it a wide berth. Just the sound of it was unnerving, and I knew we would soon have to navigate within feet of the deadly shoal. The moon was a quarter way through its journey when we turned to starboard and reefed the sails. Speed would be our enemy now. To that effect, I had the men rig one of the foresails as a sea anchor to slow our approach.

I was growing impatient with our progress, but it was the only way to ensure the safety of the ship and crew. If this was a fool's errand, then my short career as a captain would be at an end.

The lead came back with ten fathoms and Mason called for the sails to be furled. *The Panther* slowed, but it was now caught in the swell. The force of the waves slung us toward the reef, increasing in size as we moved into ever-shallower water.

I climbed back into the rigging to orient myself. We had only minutes to find the wreck and anchor or we would have to waste valuable time turning around and trying again. I could tell that many of the men were already nervous.

A large wave crashed nearby. I was just about to call to Mason to change course when I saw something strange in the water. There was a dull glow coming from the depths. "Drop anchor," I yelled.

The boat was alive now, the silence broken by the anchor hitting the water. We swung one hundred and eighty degrees as it grabbed, and I could feel the vibration in the rigging when the hook set. The moon was high in the sky now, the perfect time to get to the business at hand. The tide would be slack and I was hoping the moonlight would penetrate the seas. As Mason and I moved to the skiff, I ordered a half dozen men into the water to search for the weighted line we had discarded earlier.

I felt a twinge of fear creep up my spine when they placed the head gear on me. It was dark and cold inside the leather helmet, and the facemask was fogged up and of no use. I was virtually blind when they handed me the line, but I felt slightly better when I felt the first surge of fresh air from the pump.

I had taught myself to breathe deeply on my previous dives, but as I drifted down the line in the black water, I started to panic and gasped for air. In my confusion I lost count of the knots and, before I knew it, I crashed to the deck, my head aching from the pressure in my ears.

I sat on the *Ludlow*'s deck, trying to pull myself together. A tug on the rope brought me back to reality and I remembered I was supposed to signal when I hit bottom.

I gave the signal and shifted the glass in front of my face. The darkness was overwhelming, the glow I had seen from the surface no longer visible. I would have to feel my way to the treasure. Fortunately I had left the line by the ballast pile. I felt around in a circle until I found one of the weights. My eyes had adjusted enough to barely see the deck now, but my sight was limited to three feet at the most.

From the blackness, I felt a surge in the water, and then another. Instinctively, I covered myself, preparing for the attack I thought was coming, but then realized it was our men. Mason had four men waiting for my signal and had sent each with a section of cargo net attached to a line that led to the ship.

I took the bundle from the first diver and felt him kick off the deck and ascend. I piled a half dozen of the coral-encrusted castings into the net and pulled hard on the line, then repeated the procedure several more times until the pile was gone. Finally, I grabbed the bottom of the last net and rode it to the surface, relieved when I could see the moon glimmering through the water.

When I boarded the *Panther*, Mason and Rhames clapped me on the back, and I watched the crew work frantically to secure the treasure. Although we weren't safe yet, looking at the faces of the rescued slaves as they handled the silver they had a share in brought a smile to my face.

I knew by now the captain of the frigate would have secured the pinnace and would likely be coming back by this route, disappointed and fearful of Bodden's wrath, but either way, we needed to weigh anchor and get underway.

The tide had turned, making it easier to escape our mooring, and Mason called for the topsails the minute the anchor was clear of the water. The ship swung to the northeast, caught the wind and soon we were making good time.

The treasure was now secure and the first rays of dawn highlighted the whitecaps as we slid through the waves at a favorable angle. I climbed to my spot in the rigging and glanced back at the island, now almost invisible on the horizon. For a moment, I thought I caught a glimpse of the frigate in the distance, but we were far to sea and the sun would be in their eyes. I knew we were free.

The rigging was a comfortable place to dream and think, a place where no one bothered me. I stared out to sea, wondering what was next for us, when I felt Shayla next to me. I put my arm around her and leaned in to kiss her.

## ABOUT THE AUTHOR

Always looking for a new location or adventure to write about, Steven Becker can usually be found on or near the water. He splits his time between Tampa and the Florida Keys - paddling, sailing, diving, fishing or exploring.

Find out more by visiting www.stevenbeckerauthor.com or contact me directly at booksbybecker@gmail.com.

facebook.com/stevenbecker.books
instagram.com/stevenbeckerauthor

**Get my starter library First Bite for Free!
when you sign up for my newsletter**

http://eepurl.com/-obDj

First Bite contains the first book in several of Steven Becker's series:

**Get them now (http://eepurl.com/-obDj)**

## Mac Travis Adventures: The Wood's Series

It's easy to become invisible in the Florida Keys. Mac Travis is laying low: Fishing, Diving and doing enough salvage work to pay his bills. Staying under the radar is another matter altogether. An action-packed thriller series featuring plenty of boating, SCUBA diving, fishing and flavored with a generous dose of Conch Republic counterculture.

### Check Out The Series Here

★★★★★ *Becker is one of those, unfortunately too rare, writers who very obviously knows and can make you feel, even smell, the places he writes about. If you love the Keys, or if you just want to escape there for a few enjoyable hours, get any of the Mac Travis books - and a strong drink*

★★★★★*This is a terrific series with outstanding details of Florida, especially the Keys. I can imagine myself riding alone with Mac through every turn. Whether it's out on a boat or on an island....I'm there*

## Kurt Hunter Mysteries: The Backwater Series

Biscayne Bay is a pristine wildness on top of the Florida Keys. It is also a stones throw from Miami and an area notorious for smuggling. If there's nefarious activity in the park, special agent Kurt Hunter is sure to stumble across it as he patrols the backwaters of Miami.

**Check it out the series here**

★★★★★ *This series is one of my favorites. Steven Becker is a genius when it comes to weaving a plot and local color with great characters. It's like dessert, I eat it first*

★★★★★ *Great latest and greatest in the series or as a stand alone. I don't want to give up the plot. The characters are more "fleshed out" and have become "real." A truly believable story in and about Florida and Floridians.*

## Tides of Fortune

### What do you do when you're labeled a pirate in the nineteenth century Caribbean

Follow the adventures of young Captain Van Doren as he and his crew try to avoid the hangman's noose. With their uniques mix of skills, Nick and company roam the waters of the Caribbean looking for a safe haven to spend their wealth. But, the call "Sail on the horizon" often changes the best laid plans.

### Check out the series here

★★★★★ *This is a great book for those who like me enjoy "factional" books. This is a book that has characters that actually existed and took place in a real place(s). So even though it isn't a true story, it certainly could be. Steven Becker is a terrific writer and it certainly shows in this book of action of piracy, treasure hunting,ship racing etc*

## The Storm Series

Meet contract agents John and Mako Storm. The father and son duo are as incompatible as water and oil, but necessity often forces them to work together. This thriller series has plenty of international locations, action, and adventure.

**Check out the series here**

★★★★★ *Steven Becker's best book written to date. Great plot and very believable characters. The action is non-stop and the book is hard to put down. Enough plot twists exist for an exciting read. I highly recommend this great action thriller.*

★★★★★ *A thriller of mega proportions! Plenty of action on the high seas and in the Caribbean islands. The characters ran from high tech to divers to agents in the field. If you are looking for an adrenalin rush by all means get Steven Beckers new E Book*

## The Will Service Series

If you can build it, sail it, dive it, and fish it—what's left. Will Service: carpenter, sailor, and fishing guide can do all that. But trouble seems to find him and it takes all his skill and more to extricate himself from it.

### Check out the series here

★★★★★ *I am a sucker for anything that reminds me of the great John D. MacDonald and Travis McGee. I really enjoyed this book. I hope the new Will Service adventure is out soon, and I hope Will is living on a boat. It sounds as if he will be. I am now an official Will Service fan. Now, Steven Becker needs to ignore everything else and get to work on the next Will Service novel*

★★★★★ *If you like Cussler you will like Becker! A great read and an action packed thrill ride through the Florida Keys!*

Printed in Great Britain
by Amazon